A VAMPIRE IN A PEAR TREE

A Ravenfall Novella

KATIE MACALISTER

FAT CAT BOOKS

www.katiemacalister.com
Cover by Croco Designs
Formatting by Racing Pigeon Productions

AUTHOR'S NOTE

In 2024, I released *All the Jingle Ladies*, a holiday short story that featured dragons, vampires, and polters. It was basically a fun way to push the mingled paranormal storylines a bit further while also having a holiday flavored catch up.

This year, I decided to address the issue of the missing vampire thane, as mentioned in *Axegate Walk*, the first in the Ravenfall series.

Because I love you, my charming reader, I've included *All the Jingle Ladies* in this print volume (also because it was too short to publish in print on its own), which I hope you will adore as much as I do.

I really love writing these stories where we get to look at not only new characters, but also catch up with all your favorite characters.

Enjoy the holiday shenanigans!

Katie Mac
November, 2025

CONTENTS

ALL THE JINGLE LADIES 11

A VAMPIRE IN A PEAR TREE 67

ALL THE JINGLE LADIES
A HOLIDAY OTHERWORLD
ADVENTURE SHORT STORY

ONE
AISLING

MATES UNION GROUP CHAT

ME

Holiday greetings from the depths of Hungary! As my kids loudly informed me this morning, we are at T-minus ten days until Christmas, which means we're seven days away from the Sarkany—and subsequent holiday party—at Ysolde's, and much as I love Christmas, I'm really looking forward to the dragon get-together. For one, I can't wait to see Dragonwood decorated for Christmas. And for another, I've really missed you guys during the last couple of months.

YSOLDE

Pavel and I are going all out on the Sarkany dinner. I thought it would be fun to do a Festival of Seven Fishes theme, but I was informed—with many marked looks and wrinkled noses—that dragons aren't very fond of seafood, and prefer red meat. Pavel suggested a traditional English prime rib, Yorkshire pudding, braised red cabbage, Brussel sprouts with bacon and brown sugar, herb-roasted potatoes, and a port cranberry sauce that I can personally attest is to die for. Naturally, I agreed to his suggestion.

MAY

Naturally. Also, can I say that you finding Baltic (and Pavel) again is the best thing that's happened to the dragonkin?

ME

It so is. Although as a result of that dinner, I'll to have to use the new fancy high tech treadmill that Drake has put at the top of his Christmas list.

SOPHEA

Mmmm. It'll be worth it, though.

BEE

Wait...Drake feels he needs to exercise? Did he suddenly get a dad bod? Because the last time we saw you guys, all the wyverns were looking pretty damned good. I asked Constantine if all wyverns had to be drop-dead gorgeous like him. He just looked pleased but didn't answer.

ME

Drake is just as deliciously buff as ever—although I think we can agree Baltic has the best six pack of all the wyverns—but he does love electronics and related gadgets, and since he's so hard to buy for, I'm willing to take any suggestion he makes.

What are you guys getting your respective wyvern or mate?

MAY

Unfortunately, Gabriel has learned from Drake's techy addiction, and is a right royal pain in the ass when it comes to keeping him from just buying anything he wants. But this year, I've managed to get him a jet ski that he knows nothing about, so it'll be a true surprise.

ME

You do know that water is the green dragon element, yes?

MAY

Oh, I know full well the silver dragons think water is something to bear instead of enjoy, but I'm confident that zipping around in a speedy jet ski will drop that objection to nil.

YSOLDE

I imagine so! That's quite the present, as well. I had to put a moratorium on self indulgent shopping between the months of September and Christmas. It was the only way I could keep all the boys from eliminating their wish lists before December hit, but even so, I've only gotten two things for Baltic: a gift certificate, and a gazebo with tinted windows so you can't see what's going on inside.

MAY

LOL!

ME

An excellent idea. What is the gift cert for? Something Baltic wouldn't normally get himself, I'm guessing.

YSOLDE

It's to my favorite sex shop. You know, the one the First Dragon visited when I was there with Constantine.

BEE

Why do I not know this story? Where is that wyvern of mine? Be right back...

SOPHEA

Smart thinking on the shopping moratorium. I'll do that with my family next year. Rowan and I aren't really doing anything but minor presents since we're saving for a house in France so we can be closer to Bee and Aoife and everyone else. Oh, while I'm thinking of it, an update on our holiday travel plans: we're going to travel from St. Petersburg with Aoife and Kostya, so we'll arrive in England the day before the Sarkany. We're excited to see you all again. I gather Rowan's been getting a lot of dude advice from the wyverns, and he can't wait to show everyone how he can shift into and out of dragon form without any trouble now.

CHARITY

#dragongoals

ME

Indeed. Will the First Dragon and you be attending the Sarkany, Charity?

CHARITY

I will, but the First Dragon is off trying to find his oldest son...again...so he will not be available.

ME

His oldest...oh, the firstborn of the firstborn, the one who Baltic went to fetch? I thought they found him in Arizona?

YSOLDE

Baltic did, yes. And offered aid, which was spurned. Then some stuff happened about which Baltic is keeping very mum, which he knows irritates me, but you know how the boys are when they don't feel like forthcoming with the bare minimum of information that would keep a beloved mate from going stark, staring mad.

ME

Are you panting with outrage right now, Ysolde?

YSOLDE

No, but only because Baltic and Pavel are off with the kids to find a suitable fir tree to fell. Holland and I were laid low with Anduin's cold, so we're both bundled up with hot toddies while the others are being rugged and festive. Or in Brom's case, rugged and angsty. Oh, Holland says hello, and please forgive him for not responding, but he's in a toddy stupor and keeps falling asleep after asking me what you all are saying.

MAY

Do I sense romance gossip incoming? Please tell me you have something to share, because Gabriel and I are addicted to what he's calling the Pixie and Brom telenovela, and I promised him I'd get any updates that are forthcoming.

BEE

Back after hearing about the sex shop. I'm getting Constantine a gaming laptop for Christmas, and we're giving Gary the disembodied head a game machine with custom printed controllers so he can play more easily. BRB again...putting the baby down for a nap so I can catch up on the teen romance goss. Go ahead and start without me.

YSOLDE

There's not too much to tell, to be honest. Well, not too much to tell NOW. I suspect that after Christmas, there will be much, assuming Brom says I can share, which he usually does because it makes him feel like a main character. Honestly, I don't remember being as dramatic as he is when I was his age, but the emoting! The fiery (literally) gestures! The slamming doors, and demands for a private jet to take him to the west coast of the US, and outrageous statements about no one understanding what he has to go through just to exist.

ME

It sounds exhausting, and also like I'd better invest now in a solid CBD gummies company, because I have

a feeling the teen dragon drama isn't going to be limited to just Brom.

MAY

Again, I'd like to repeat that Gabriel's nieces, who
stay with us a couple of times a year, are perfectly
charming and well-behaved.

In fact, the oldest of them, Durra, will be with us
for a few months after the new year. Evidently, she's
interested in becoming an heir, which of course worries
Gabriel to death.

PHYLLIDA

I hate being the new kid. What's an heir other than
the obvious meaning? I'm having a portrait painted of
Bastian and me for his Christmas present, and Seawright—my scribe—will be getting an online writing
course she's been lusting after.

MAY

In this instance, the heir is the next wyvern of the
sept. Most wyverns pick their successor, and since his
nieces have one mortal parent, they could all be wyverns.
Only Durra is interested in the position, which alter-
nately pleases and terrifies Gabriel.

CHARITY

I thought Gabriel's mother was a powerful shaman?

MAY

Kawaa is very powerful, but shamans—for some
reason I don't quite understand—are considered mortal, even though they are reborn to live again when their
bodies die.

CHARITY

Gotcha.

PHYLLIDA

That makes sense why Gabriel would be concerned.
Also, Ysolde, my commiseration on the teen drama.

YSOLDE

I will be sure to reciprocate if you and Bastian have children.

PHYLLIDA

I have a junior scribe, third class, bound to me for life, and that's pretty much tantamount to the angstiest of teens.

ME

But what's up with Uriah? That is, why has the FD gone to find him? He's sent Baltic to do it twice, yes? Why does the first firstborn keep going missing?

CHARITY

It's Yrian. The First Dragon pronounces it EAR-ian, and I assume he knows his own child's name.

ME

My apologies. Why does Yrian keep disappearing?

ME

Hello? Did I delete the chat group by mistake again? Dammit, I didn't touch anything in the settings this time...

YSOLDE

Sorry, I was giving Charity a chance to be forth-coming with information, since we all know that the wyverns aren't going to offer any information unless we threaten them with dire repercussions.

CHARITY

Alas, I am unable to fill you up with info.

YSOLDE

Unable or unwilling?

CHARITY

Does it really matter?

YSOLDE

Yes. Did the First Dragon tell you what's going on with Yrian?

YSOLDE

Charity?

CHARITY

Yes and no. Yes, he said his son had...challenges... that were not going very well, but that it wasn't surprising. Then he said something about Baltic not being helpful, and that he'd have to go attend to things himself. He wasn't very happy about that, by the way.

YSOLDE

What else is new? I figured he had asked Baltic something outrageous last month, but the love of my life wouldn't tell me just what it was.

He simply said it was beyond his abilities, and he wouldn't put us at risk to dig his brother out of whatever hole he was hiding in.

ME

Ouch—and that's no reflection on Baltic, but more a commentary on his brother having some sorts of trouble. Let me know if the Green Dragons can be of help, although I'm sure the FD would tell Drake if he wanted that.

CHARITY

I will pass along the offer when I hear from the First Dragon. I'm recording a bunch of songs for him for his Christmas present. As you can imagine, it's hard to buy for a demigod, and the only thing he said he wished he had was me with him when he was away. This is the closest thing I could do.

ME

Holy crapballs! I had no idea the First Dragon was so romantic.

MAY

Seriously. What a sweet thing to say.

YSOLDE

I'll give him that. It is basically the perfect compliment.

CHARITY

I like to think he's the First Dragon for a reason—he has all the moves. As for the Sarkany and following party, should I bring something?

MAY

Dragon's blood wine is always good. That and champagne is usually what we bring for Ysolde's shindigs.

YSOLDE

Both are welcome, but beyond that, I believe we have enough food for an army. And since Brom will be away in Hawaii for the week, we shouldn't have to fight him and his endless appetite for the goodies.

AOIFE

Brom is going to Hawaii? For Christmas? That sounds heavenly! I'm going to mention that to Kostya for next year. I'm not saying I don't like St. Petersburg, but it's cold enough outside to freeze the warts off a toad. Also, I'm getting Kostya an easel and set of paints. Evidently, Constantine told Bee that Kostya used to paint way back when they were widdle dragons, and I thought it was something fun he might like to try again. He's taking me to Tibet as my present, so we can go examine some aerie place where he was held captive.

PHYLLIDA

I don't want to say that's an odd choice of presents, because you do you, but an aerie prison? That doesn't sound like much fun.

AOIFE

Tibet does, though, and Kostya has promised me all the bad dragons are gone from the aerie, so it should be safe.

ME

Sounds like a fun adventure! Just be sure to wear good boots, because it's a hell of a climb. But what's this about Brom not being with you for the festivities, Ysolde?

YSOLDE

Didn't I tell you all? Karma, Adam, and Pixie are going to Hawaii for Christmas, and evidently Pixie invited Brom to join them, and he went straight to Baltic, who immediately bought him a plane ticket, and then tried very hard for three days to get on my good side after I found out.

ME

Who tried to get on your good side? Brom or Baltic?

YSOLDE

Both.

ME

Oh man, I imagine that didn't go over well.

YSOLDE

I am nothing if not a reasonable person, and after some discussions with Baltic—and much fiery stomping around with waving arms by Brom—I decided that Baltic was right, and this was a good chance for Brom to have a little independence while still including responsible adults nearby.

So yes, he leaves two days before the Sarkany, and will be gone for a week.

I've already offered to pay for a few month's therapy for Karma and Adam since being in close contact with Brom and Pixie is likely to push them to hitherto unforeseen limits of patience.

AOIFE

I have a little update. I texted Kostya about Yrian to

see what he knew, and he said the only thing he heard was that Yrian was the founder of the black sept.

After several minutes of telling him to stop being such a drama llama about me asking him to share dragon lore, he finally added that the first group of black dragons didn't make it, and the sept went dormant until one of the green sept's descendants took up the mantel of wyvern, and got it running again.

BEE

Holy cheese and crackers! I had no idea that sort of thing went on. I'll try to pin down Constantine for more information.

MAY

Same. I have a feeling Gabriel knows more than he's sharing. He keeps dimpling at me, and we all know what effect that has.

YSOLDE

It has you lusting after his manly self to the point where you forget about what information you were trying to gain?

MAY

Bingo!

ME

I've said it before, and I'll say it again: distraction, thy name is wyvern. Right, I think we're all caught up to date, so I'd better get moving before the kids paint the kitchen with food coloring. We're decorating cookies this afternoon, and I just saw Jim trotting in their direction with a piping bag filled with red frosting in its mouth, so I'd best go avert *that* disaster in the making. See you all at the Sarkany!

TWO
KARMA

"Did you catch all the imps?" I had intended on greeting my father in a more affectionate manner, but since he had, less than six hours after we flew out of Seattle, managed to not only release my eight imps from their playpen, but then allowed them outside because he thought they needed exercise. The result was all eight ended up frolicking in a small, scum-filled pond, which meant I was less polite than normal. "Please tell me you found them all. It's far too cold for them to be running around the garden. And don't use the bathtub in the main bath, since they can climb out of it. Use the garden tub off my room. Remember to test the water temp first. It should be body temperature for them. Oh, and you can use a little of my shampoo as bubble bath liquid. It doesn't have any chemicals that would harm them."

"Karma, honey, you sound like you don't trust me at all. Of course I got all your imps back in, and yes, I hosed them off in your tub, and put them back into their playpen. They're yammering non-stop to each other, so you can stop worrying."

"An imp foster mother never stops worrying," I said before I realized just what my mouth thought was a sane thought to share. I rubbed my forehead, shifted my sunglasses when the movement sent a shaft of sunlight to pierce straight into my brain, and added quickly, "Pretend I didn't say that. Just don't let them out of their pen except to go to bed. We're only going to be gone for a week, and that new playpen has room for them to exercise without risking them swallowing whatever runoff drains into that pond."

"You worry too much. Is Adam there?" Dad asked.

I glanced across the airport lobby to where the tall, curly-haired, blue-eyed polter of my dreams stood next to a female a foot and a half shorter.

Pixie, my foster daughter, had adopted a hairstyle that reminded me of a particularly untidy stork's nest, complete with spiky bits that flicked in an annoyed manner when she moved. "It's not often you see hair actually look pissed at the world, but somehow, she's pulled it off."

"Who, Pixie?"

"Yes. And yes, Adam is still here. He hasn't run away from us, if that's what you were wondering."

"Of course I'm not. You two are perfect for each other. A nice poltergeist boy—"

"Half-polter," I corrected, noting the emergence of a wad of people. Evidently the flight from LA had arrived. Pixie stood on her tip toes to scan the crowd.

"And you're a wonderful polter girl—"

Another clutch of people arrived, but I didn't see the tall, lanky nineteen year old I was expecting. "Mom would not appreciate you forgetting that she was, and still is, very much a human, which makes me also half-polter."

"—so why would he leave you? Dammit. One of them switched the channel to something with a bunch of jumping kids. I was going to watch curling."

"They love sports so long as you tell them what's going on, but I told you not to give them the remote. They get too excited with more than an hour of the Disney channel, and that tends to lead to them weeing on the remote. Oh good, there he is. Crisis averted."

"Young love, eh, Karma?"

I ignored my father, smiling as Brom, the newest member of the light dragons, dropped his bag to envelope Pixie in a bear hug. Pixie, for her part, had adopted what I recognized as her (very studied) nonchalant demeanor, but that didn't stand a chance against Brom's enthusiasm and what I was coming to view as his own form of joie d'vivre.

"Eh, Karma?"

"Gotta go, Dad. Adam is hovering in a manner that tells me his Dadness wants to nip any public displays of affection in the bud, while at the same time trying to give Pixie space to be herself. Love you. Don't let them out again! I'll call again in a few days."

"Don't be so caught up in the kids that you and Adam can't have a trial honeymoon," Dad said quickly as I was about to click off the call.

"We are not getting married, as I've told you twelve times in the last two months. Bye!"

He sputtered a protest that I ended with the call. Before I had taken more than six steps, Brom strode over to stop before me, making a bow that was both awkward and oddly touching. The dragons, as I well knew, clung to the old ways in many things, and respectful greetings were at the top of their list. They all bowed beautifully, a trait that sadly escaped polters, although

Adam and I had a very giggly evening a few months back while Pixie was off for a sleepover, during which we practiced bowing so we wouldn't shame our fellow polters the next time we met with dragons. Much wine was involved, but a memory of the rest of the evening had me wondering when Pixie's friend might want her over for another Stranger Things marathon.

"Karma." Brom made a bow to Adam, as well, although this one a bit choppier. "It's a pleasure to see you again. You look well. Sullivan asked me to say Merry Christmas from everyone, and that she hopes you don't go insane, but if you do, she's got you covered with therapy. All you have to do is send her the provider, and she'll take care of the rest."

He looked so earnest that I fought back the giggle that rose at his idea of a greeting (not to mention Ysolde's offer). I hadn't yet figured out why Brom called her Sullivan, but figured that might be a mystery to tackle while we enjoyed our vacation.

Adam's lips twitched, and he murmured something about checking on our flight to Maui before hurrying off.

"And how're the light dragons?" I asked as we moved over to a waiting area. "Baltic and your brother and the others?"

"Good," he said, his face moving into a serious expression. Another giggle rose in me, but I squashed it mercilessly. "Baltic is...well..."

"Baltic," I said with an understanding nod.

"He's intense," Pixie said, giving a little toss of the stork's nest before sitting down. Brom, I noticed, hurriedly dumped his luggage so he could take the plastic seat next to her. Pixie stiffened when his leg touched hers, but she looked more startled than unhappy.

We'd had a talk back in the planning stages of the vacation about consent, and what it looked like in a variety of circumstances, and how emotions could cloud issues, and I felt, on the whole, that she was prepared for a romantic relationship.

Birth control, check, I thought, running through the list that had plagued me in the middle of the night. *Consent talk, check. Visit to Planned Parenthood for any remaining questions and concerns, check.*

A familiar panic filled me. I turned away from Pixie and Brom while they chatted about their respective flights, what movies they watched, who annoyed them on the flights, and why it was stupid that they could drink in Europe, but not in the US.

ME

I'd never been a parent before! Here I am trying to guide a troubled seventeen-year-old through her first romantic relationship. Given my former marriage, who am I to try to give her advice?

ADAM

Having another panic attack, are we?

ME

Of course I am! Why the hell did I think this was at all a reasonable idea?

ADAM

Because you're a good foster mom, and you want Pixie to grow up into a confident woman like you. Well, normally confident. When you don't get freaked out at kids being kids.

ME

These kids could get pregnant. Or diseased. Or get into kinky stuff that isn't good for their self-confidence. Or any number of other horrors. How on earth did you get through this with Vanessa?

ADAM

Whisky. Vast quantities of it over the years. Also, she didn't go completely insane between fifteen and nineteen. Just mostly insane.

ME

I'd sigh a heavy, heartfelt sigh, but the kids would hear me. When do we board the next plane?

ADAM

Another hour. Breathe through the panic. I'll be there shortly. I just have to call in to my Watch supervisor.

"Karma?"

"Hmm?" I looked up, realizing that Brom had asked a question. "Sorry, I was texting Adam. He says we can't board the plane for another hour, so I guess we'll just stay here."

Pixie gave a toss of her stork's nest, the tendrils vibrating angrily. "I said that we were hungry, and Brom said there's a place to eat on the other side of the terminal. We're going to get some lunch."

I ignored the fact that she made a statement rather than asking if they could go, aware that there was a fine balance to be had between independence and folly. "It's only ten and we had breakfast on the plane, but I imagine Brom is feeling some jetlag, so if you guys want to grab a bite to eat, that's fine with me. Just be back here in half an hour, OK? We don't want to miss the flight to Maui."

"We'll be back in time," Brom reassured me as they both got to their feet. "I've never been surfing before, and Pavel—he's Baltic's best friend—says it's not that hard to do, although later Baltic told me that Pavel breaks his nose every time he tries to surf, so I'm not sure how accurate he is. But it can't be that hard. Pixie and I are going to try it."

Pixie, once again, looked momentarily startled, but she simply nodded the nest at his statement, and the two of them slouched their way down the terminal to where the fast food places lurked.

ME

Again, why are we doing this? It seems like the height of folly now that we're here.

ADAM

It'll be wonderful. Relax. Also, as I said, whisky helps.

I tried a bit of meditation, but the hard chair, the steady stream of people passing by, and my worry over the unknown made it useless to try to relax.

YSOLDE

Brom tells me he's landed safely in Hawaii and met up with you all. I've told him that while yes, he is technically an adult, he is to defer to you and Adam if any sticky situations arise. We'll assume they won't, but alas, I know my child. Ever since he became a dragon, drama seems to stalk him.

ME

Merry Christmas to you all, as well! And I'm sure everything will be fine. What could happen in a tropical paradise like Hawaii?

"Famous last words," I murmured to myself as I tucked away my phone, and headed over to the terminal for our next flight.

Several hours later I strolled out of the hotel lobby, and into a vast expanse of beach.

DAD

Did you get to your hotel? There's been an incident.

ME

What sort of an incident? Is one of the imps injured? Is there blood?

DAD

What sort of a person do you take me for? I'm not the sort of monster who would allow an imp under my watch to get injured! Besides, it's not that sort of an incident. It's Cardea. She refuses to come out of the pantry.

ME

What? She's been happily decorating the spare bedroom the last few weeks. What happened to send her back to the pantry?

"Judging by your frown, I'm guessing there's a problem?" Adam asked as passed me with a bag of supplies he felt were necessary for the hour we were going to spend on the beach watching the sunset.

"Just my dad," I muttered, tapping furiously on my phone.

ME

What did you say to her? Dammit, Dad! We've worked for the last six months with Cardea's therapist to get her out of the pantry. What happened?

DAD

I told her it wasn't healthy for her to be stuck in the house all the time, and tried to get her to take a drive with me and the imps. She locked herself into the pantry.

"What did Matthew do now?"

I looked up at Adam's cocked eyebrow of questioning. "Messed with Cardea to the point where she's locked herself in the pantry."

He flinched. "Ouch. She's been doing so well. Still, she is the goddess of doors, and if her agoraphobia is raging, I expect she's more comfortable locked away."

"She's a goddess of door hinges and thresholds," I corrected, then took a deep breath, texted a few choice words to my father about leaving her alone for the rest of our trip, and put my phone in my pocket before I did more. "Right. Shall we watch the romantic sunset on the romantic beach with romantic wine and cheeses?"

"I nixed the cheese," he said, holding up a bottle of wine. "I figured a cheese board isn't ideal when sitting on the sand. What the hell?"

It was Adam's turn to get an annoying text, and with a muttered comment about the Watch knowing better than to disturb him for the first vacation he'd taken in a year, he set down the bag and blanket, and moved off to deal with work.

"What are you doing? Is that wine? We can't drink wine here. We could if we were in Europe. The US has a lot to learn from Europe. Are there sand fleas? Brom said there were sand fleas when he and the dragons went to somewhere in the Caribbean. Will my mosquito spray work on sand fleas? Where's Adam going? I thought you were going to watch the sunset while Brom and I go to the club? You said we could go to the club because it's inside the hotel complex! You can't change your mind now!"

"Whoa," I said, holding up a hand and slanting a glance upward to where Pixie stood next to me, all of her hands on her hips. Because the hotel we were staying at catered only to Otherworld clientele, she had dispensed with the glamour that kept her four-armed appearance from startling mortals. "That was a lot. Let's start with the most objectionable first."

"Objectionable!" she said, slapping two hands on her legs while the others gesticulated wildly. "I'm not objectionable!"

"No, you aren't, but acting like a petulant child by jumping to conclusions isn't going to foster the sense of trust you want us to have in you. I'm not changing my mind, Pixie. You and Brom are welcome to enjoy the amenities at the hotel, including the club, so long as you tell us where you are going. So, a little less of the accusations, please, and more of the sharing of information. Are you going to have dinner with us, or did you want to go elsewhere? Adam said that he's willing to let Brom drive the rental car so long as he's very careful. It will mean wearing a glamour if you go off the property, though."

She made a face. Of late, she'd been railing against having to wear glamours when out in public, but since it would be another decade, at least, before the first of her two extraneous arms dropped off, she'd just have to get used to it. "There's a micro pub speakeasy thing in the basement that we could go to."

I pursed my lips.

She gave a dramatic roll of her eyes, slapped her hands on her thighs again, and said as she pulled out her phone, "Fine! We won't have any alcohol. They have food there, too, and music and sometimes dancing and a trivia contest that Brom says we can ace, because he's a dragon, and dragons know stuff."

"Sounds like a good time," I said, not pointing out the fact that Brom had been a dragon for a year. "Curfew at 2am, please."

"That's, like, ridiculous," she said absently, tapping on her phone. "You said we could do stuff by ourselves because the hotel was safe."

"It is, but you are still only seventeen, and I think 2am is reasonable. Do you have your room card?"

"Yeah." She made a face at her phone. "Mariah says you're infantilizing me."

I blinked in confusion, then my teen translator kicked in. "I'm sorry your bestie thinks I'm infantilizing you, but I assure you that were I to do so, your curfew would be 9pm. Where's Brom?"

She gestured toward a patio area. "His mom called. Mariah says I should test Brom to see if he's worthy of me. She says Lou tested her boyfriend, and he failed. He totally kissed Mariah when she tested him."

"Tested him?" I asked.

"You know! To see if he'd cheat on Lou. That's so scummy! If my boyfriend ever kissed anyone else, I'd torment him for years."

Luckily, Adam finished his texting before I was called upon to comment on Pixie's statement, so instead I told her, "Have fun at the speakeasy. Call or text if you need us, and if you leave the hotel complex, I want you back on the grounds by midnight. I don't mind you wandering the complex late at night, but I've heard too many things about drunken mortal tourists to have you guys off site."

Pixie snorted derisively, and muttered a few things under her breath that I thought it better to not hear, then stormed off in her usual manner.

"I'm sure she didn't take the curfew well," Adam said as he sat down next to me on the blanket I'd spread out. The beach held scattered clumps of people obviously there to see the spectacular sunset, but we were private enough that we could talk without being overheard. "Did Brom talk to you?"

"About what?" I asked, musing on how to talk to Pixie about taking relationship advice from her friends. "He thanked me again for inviting him on the trip, but I took that to be Ysolde driving good manners into his head before he left. Did he say anything to you?"

A martyred expression crawled across Adam's handsome face. His eyes, which were a pale blue that never failed to make my stomach feel wobbly, gazed out at the sea. "What didn't he say would be more to point. He pulled me aside when you and Pixie were unpacking, and gave me an earnest speech about how now that he was a dragon, I didn't have to protect Pixie or him. According to him, no one messes with dragons, and thus, he will take over the job of keeping Pixie safe, and we can sit back and relax."

"Oh lord," I said, feeling a similar martyred feeling stealing over me. "He didn't really say all that, did he?"

"Word for word," Adam said, stretching out his legs and opening one of the bottles of wine. "I told him that I appreciated the offer of help, and that I'd count on his assistance if it was needed, but that I didn't expect an attack by imps, or murderous spirits, or any of the other horrible things that have happened in the last year."

"I really want to say, 'Famous last words,' to that statement, but I have a horrible presentiment that if I do so, I'll simply be summoning trouble, so instead, let's just toast to a quiet, uncomplicated evening, and fun time later in our room's massive shower."

He waggled his eyebrows in a way that made me feel giggly, and I forced myself to enjoy the moment, and let go of my worries for a while.

There was a more formal restaurant that Adam and I dressed up to visit, which also made me feel a bit giddy.

"You know that my dad wants us to get married," I told him as we were seated next to a window with a glorious view of the ocean.

"I do indeed know. He suggests it weekly, if not daily," Adam said, perusing the menu. I made a face at the ocean. My silence had him glancing up and shooting me a speculative look. "Am I to assume that you've changed your mind?"

"No." I shook my head at the waves. "Honestly, I don't really see the need for it. I was married for more than ten years to Spider, and that was a hellish nightmare I don't ever want to repeat."

It was Adam's turn to be silent. I dragged my gaze from the water to see a question in his eyes.

"No, I do not equate you with Spider. What we have is real. It's my lack of self-confidence at twenty that led me into a marriage I will regret until the end of my days. You, on the other hand, are wonderful. I want us to be together...just not married." I put my hand on his, giving it a squeeze before I searched his expression, worried that I'd hurt his feelings. "I thought you felt the same way I did about marriage, but maybe *you've* changed *your* mind?"

"I haven't, as a matter of fact," he said, relaxing a smidgen, and lifting my hand to kiss it, a gesture that never failed to give me a shiver of pleasure. "I've never been much for it after my own experience, and although I think we'd probably be fine married, I don't see a reason to pursue it unless you want to."

"We're on the same page, then," I said, relaxing again.

My phone pinged with a text while we were waiting for our starters.

PIXIE

Our team is in the lead for trivia!

ME

Congratulations. Good luck with the rest of the event. Is the speakeasy nice? Adam and I may want to visit it.

PIXIE

YOU SAID WE COULD GO HERE BY OURSELVES!

ME

Calm down, Shouty McShouterson. I meant another time, not tonight when you and Brom are having fun.

PIXIE

Oh. OK, but don't change your mind. There's a bachelorette party that's broken up into five teams, and we're beating the crap out of them because they're drunk. We don't need competition like Adam taking away our glorious win.

ME

I will be sure to tell him you think that he—and evidently, only he—poses a threat to your trivia crown.

"Are they having fun?" Adam asked, buttering a deliciously soft dinner roll.

"Sounds like it. They're winning at trivia. I am regretting getting Pixie her own room now, rather than getting us a suite. Who knows what they'll get up to since they each have a room."

"You know full well what they will get up to, and you've prepared Pixie for any trouble. I assume Brom's folks did the same, since I'm willing to bet the last thing Ysolde and Baltic want are grandkids running under foot. Relax, Karma. Pixie may seem heedless to you, but she's done a lot of emotional growing in the time she's been with you."

"That is true," I said, and once again, forced myself to push away the worries and enjoy my time with the most alluring of all polters.

That is, I enjoyed it until a horrible thought struck me.

I pushed away my bread plate when my stomach threatened to turn over.

"What's wrong?" he asked.

I stared at him, my mind filled with a stream of mental images. "What if Pixie wants to marry Brom?"

Adam shrugged and picked up another roll. "What if she does? He seems like a nice boy, and we're friendly enough with his folks. She could do worse."

"My objection isn't to Brom, himself. I like him. I like Ysolde, and although Baltic is a bit intimidating, it's clear he loves his family, and would do anything for them. My problem is what if she wants to marry him *now?*"

Miserably, I poked at the bread plate with a knife bearing a smear of butter.

"Now? She's only seventeen."

"Next year, then, when she's legally an adult." I waved the bread knife around, my paranoia running a bit wild. "I can just see her being swept away on a romantic idea of marriage to a dragon, and eloping, only to return triumphant to tell me she was moving to England to live with Brom's family. Ysolde won't just kill me, she'll send Baltic after all of us!

Adam laughed at my admittedly dramatic statement, and spent the rest of the dinner reassuring me that Pixie had more sense than that.

It wasn't until we had returned to our room, enjoyed the large shower in a way the manufacturers probably didn't consider during the design stage (or perhaps they did, in which case, I want to thank them for that sturdy marble built-in seat), and were snuggled up in bed watching one of Adam's favorite cop shows that the worrisome texts started.

PIXIE
Are you guys naked? Are you sexing?
ME
Excuse me?

PIXIE

Can I come in? I don't want to be traumatized if you guys are going at it.

ME

I have many things to say to your last couple of comments, but since I am in a mellow mood thanks to champagne at dinner, and fancy pillow chocolates, I will hold them in. We are decently clad, yes, although we're watching TV in bed, so if you can bear to see that, then you can come in.

She must have been standing outside our door, because before I could even tell Adam we were having company, she banged on the door.

"Pixie is have some sort of a crisis," I told Adam as I padded barefoot to the door.

We were, as I'd told her, both clad in sleeping shorts, although I wore a tank top while Adam's chest was deliciously bare.

However, he slipped on a t-shirt while I greeted Pixie, since he knew she was still a bit twitchy about the physical side of our relationship.

"No Brom?" I asked, peering out when she stomped her way into our room.

"No." I thought at first she was angry about something, but Adam—whose daughter had put him through a lot during her teen years—noticed the shiny glint to her eyes before I did, and with a murmured excuse, went out to the balcony and closed the doors behind him.

"What's up?" I asked, sitting on the pale pink striped couch, patting the spot next to me.

Pixie plopped down, and was silent for a good two minutes before she finally said, "Brom doesn't like my friends."

"What do you mean he doesn't like them?" I asked, confused. "Your friends from the Home for Innocents? He hasn't met them, has he?"

"No!" Two of her hands waved around as she talked. I kept an eye on a couple of the stork's nest tendrils that seemed to be reaching out to whap me in the face as she moved. "Mariah says he's controlling me by not letting me talk to them. He can't do that to me! I don't tell him who he can talk to, so he can't tell me! Dragons are so...so...gah!"

"Brom told you that you can't talk to your friends?" My confusion deepened. "I'm surprised by that. He doesn't seem to me to be the sort of person who would tell you what you could or could not do, but if he is, then I will be having a talk with him. And his mother."

I got my phone while she said, "All I did was ask Mariah about some things, and he lost his shit!"

"That really doesn't sound like Brom. His step-dad, yes, but not him...wait a minute. What did you ask Mariah about that had him upset?"

"Just stuff," she said, but her gaze dropped, and only one hand gestured in a vague manner. "Like about what he was doing, and what I should do, and what it meant when he said things. You know. Stuff!"

I heaved as silent a sigh as I could manage, went to the balcony doors, and told Adam, "Go back to bed. Pixie and I need a little time for a talk," before taking my ward to her room.

She protested that she wasn't a child, but once she curled up on her bed, and I'd taken over the foot of it, her antagonistic mask slipped.

Her shoulders slumped as she curled up into a miserable ball of emotions and hormones. An errant tear slipped out as she said, "He said he doesn't want to be in a relationship with me! He dumped me, Karma! Over nothing!"

"Let's back up a minute, OK? No, I'm not disregarding your feelings. I know it hurts. I've been there, too. But I'm curious what it was that Brom found objectionable in your talk with your friend."

She gave a half-shrug. "Mariah told me to dump him before he dumped me. He said that was unfair, because he'd never do that to me, but Mariah has had lots of boyfriends, and she knows how they work. She said after everything I've told her about Brom, it's clear he's domineering and pushy like all the dragons, and he'll just stomp me into being what he wants, and not let me be myself, and you said I should never change for anyone but me, and that's exactly what Mariah said, only she said that Brom's the same way and he'll want me to turn into a docile dragon's mate."

Conversation with Pixie was always an experience, but after a couple of years spent with her, I was learning to pick through her words to see the underlying issues.

"In other words, you went to your friend for relationship advice, and she told you to dump Brom, and he objected?"

She nodded and sniffled back another couple of tears, using the edge of the sheet to wipe them away with an angry gesture. "He's being unreasonable."

"Is he, though?" I asked, making my voice as gentle and non-judgemental as possible. "I can tell you with complete confidence that if I went up to Adam and told him that a friend wanted me to dump him because she believed all polters were unstable, he'd be unhappy with me, and rightly so."

"Mariah says—"

"No," I said, holding up a hand to stop her. "This isn't about your friend. This is about you and Brom. Do you think Brom is a controlling, domineering person?"

"He always holds the door open for me!" she said, unfurling her person to glare at me. "And he paid for dinner and the popcorn and then I saw the cake machine in the lobby, and I was going to get us some, but he just bought two pieces before I could. That's so controlling!"

"It sounds to me like he's trying to be nice by treating you, since he knows we have a limited income, and I assume his parents have given him some sort of discretionary funds." A thought struck me, and I asked, "Did he override any of your preferences or decisions? Did he pick out food you didn't want?"

"No." She sat with a sullen expression that slowly melted into one of speculation. "He asked me what I wanted for dinner, and said if I didn't like the vegan linguine, I could get something else. And he asked me what sort of cake I wanted from the machine, and when I said I couldn't decide between the rainbow and death by chocolate, he got me both."

"That sounds like a thoughtful boyfriend," I said, managing not to stumble over the last word. Much though I thought Pixie was too young for a romantic relationship, I had a good feeling about Brom. "The best advice I can give you is to think about what you'd like. If Brom was texting a friend about you, and was told to give you the boot because you're a polter, how would you feel?"

She bristled as she pressed back into the headboard. "He wouldn't dare!"

"Mmmhmm. And yet, you basically told him that your bestie said he wasn't good for you."

"Mariah—"

"Isn't in this relationship, but you are. Pixie, I'm not telling you to ignore your friends in favor of a romantic partner, but take their advice with a grain of salt, and remember that there are some things private in a relationship."

She shot me a fast glance. "Do you keep things private with Adam? Things you don't tell me?"

I let my eyebrows rise.

Her face turned deep red, and she waved three arms at me. "Deus! Not that!"

"Yes, as a matter of fact, there are things in my relationship that I keep just between Adam and me, and no, I am not referring to anything sexual. I like to think of it as building threads of trust that bind us to each other. So while I think it's perfectly fine for you to talk about your life with your friends, just remember to give that same respect to Brom. Do you want to tell me what happened after Mariah gave you her advice?"

She did, and it took a good fifty minutes before she was in a state of relative calmness, and I felt comfortable leaving her.

But only after she asked me to see if Brom was mad at her.

ME

I wouldn't normally do this, but she's so new to this all, my heart just breaks when she cries.

ADAM

I agree that it's not wise to interfere, but this is an exceptional case. Do you want me to help?

ME

No, but I'm suddenly ravenous, so if you could get room service to bring me up a burger, I'd be delirious with joy.

ADAM

You said you were delirious with joy in the shower. Although I have to admit, a burger sounds good right now...

I had barely tapped at Brom's door before it was whipped open, and a distraught young man faced me, both arms covered in white scales.

"Does she hate me?" he asked with a throb in his voice that—like Pixie's resented tears—plucked at my heart. "Has she sent you here to tell me to leave?"

"No, nothing like that," I said, then added, "In fact, quite the opposite. She sent me to find out if you are still angry with her. I believe she wishes to explain a few things, but wasn't sure if you were receptive to that."

"Yes!" he said, and with a quick shake of his arms, dashed out of his room and down the hall to Pixie's door.

Absently, I tamped out the fire that burned merrily where he'd stood, and watched as Pixie grabbed Brom and pulled him into her room before shutting the door a bit too loudly for a hotel.

"I have zero doubts they are going to have sex," I announced to Adam a minute later, my voice ringing with drama that would do Pixie proud. "Let's just hope that condoms and birth control implants don't fail us. Oooh. Did you get mine with onions?"

"I know you love them," Adam said, whipping a napkin off the table in his best waiter move. "So long as you don't mind me putting hot sauce on mine, I can live with your onion breath."

"I brush my teeth afterwards," I protested, joining him on the balcony so we could eat while gazing at a cloudy evening. "Besides, you have onions on your burger, too."

"That's how I knew you were the one for me," he said with a sincerity that made me feel deliciously warm and squidgy inside.

Life was definitely looking up.

THREE
YSOLDE

BROM
What am I supposed to do if someone doesn't want me to be a dragon?

ME
What? Who doesn't want you to be a dragon? Adam? Karma?

BROM
Pixie. She doesn't like it when I do what Baltic says I should do.

ME
I'm not...what he told you to do? As in...sex? Did you shift? We had the discussion about how some dragons shift during an orgasm, but if that disconcerted you or scared Pixie, then I would suggest reassuring her that it's an involuntary issue, and that you will work on controlling it. Baltic, I'm sure, will help you learn better shifting control.

BROM
No, he said that being a dragon means I should protect people who are weaker than me, and Pixie is tough, but she's a girl. She doesn't like it when I protect her.

She got mad about me opening the door, saying she was fully able to open the door herself, and not to be controlling, and that I'm taking away her autonomy. I didn't think I was controlling, but I can't protect her if I let her do everything herself.

ME
Ah. There's a difference between being naturally protective—which yes, Baltic is, and he does it well, but he also knows my limits, and to not push them, much though he tries to get away with things—now I lost my train of thought. Oh, even though Baltic takes care of us, he lets us be us, right?

He lets you do things that he knows might be dangerous, but he understands that they are important to you.

He does the same for me, although sometimes I have to remind him that I'm a dragon, too, and that despite my puny T-Rex dragon form arms, I am a badass. If Pixie doesn't understand that you are simply trying to show her respect, talk to her. Tell her that you aren't trying to take away her autonomy, but that you value her, and want her to be happy.

BROM
OK.

BALTIC
What did you tell Brom?

ME
Oh, he texted you, too?

BALTIC
He said Pixie took objection to him buying her cake, and she and some friend on the phone decided he was a monster and that he wasn't good enough for her. The girl is delusional. He is a fine dragon. He will be an excellent wyvern after me.

ME

Pixie is seventeen, and thus, is unsure of herself in the relationship. That's not delusional, it's just...well, learning how to be in a relationship. Brom is in much the same situation, may I remind you. And since someone I can mention who better be coming home soon knows full well, happiness with a mate does not frequently start off with Disneyesque songs and happy cartoon birds flitting around.

BALTIC

I knew you were my mate the minute I saw you skulking around the mortal's stable.

ME

Would that be before or after you held a sword to my throat and threatened to kill me because I was not born a black dragon?

BALTIC

I don't agree with Drake when he wishes you did not regain your memory of our lives through the centuries, but I would have no complaints if you'd forget the first forty-eight hours after I took you from the mortals you claimed were your parents.

ME

Fat chance. And they *were* my parents! They simply didn't give birth to me.

Also, Karma just sent the mates group chat a picture of a gorgeous looking bleu cheese burger that she and Adam are enjoying in balmy Hawaii.

Will you be home in the next half hour? If so, can you stop at that pub that has the gourmet burgers, and get us a couple? Anduin would like chicken nuggets. Since Pavel is with you, he can consult with Holland for their dinner choice. The pub has some excellent steak pies that I know he likes.

BALTIC

They were not your parents. They simply took care of you for a bit.

ME

Not getting into it. Mostly because they've been dead for five hundred years, although I do still miss them and my sister. Yes on the burgers?

BALTIC

Do you doubt me?

ME

Never. Although sometimes Pavel gets upset when we indulge in not-so-healthy dinners...

FOUR
EFFRIJIM

Heya Amelie. I'm going to voice-to-text a letter for you to read to Cecile. I'm being all literary 'n stuff by including important things like texts, and conversations with others, and of course, my super savvy analysis of just which dragons are deranged, and which give good belly scritches (May always wins that because she uses her dragon claws, but Aisling is a close second). OK, starting now!

UNKNOWN NUMBER

Effrijim. This is my new phone, since the previous one I stole from a guard was lost in the Lake of Upside-Down Sinners.

ME

Heya, Dad. Wait, do you want me to call you Desislav instead? I mean, Desi is cool and all, but maybe you prefer Dad? I like the name Desi, though. Executive decision here: I'll call you Desi. How's mom doing? I haven't heard from you guys in a couple of months. Everything OK?

Where are you? Did you find a house in England? We're in England now, mostly because Drake has a

Sarkany here—that's a big dragon meeting—but also, Aisling prefers English Christmases over the Hungarian ones, so she and Drake trade off every year. This year it's Xmas in Ole Blighty.

ME

Also, Merry Christmas in a week. Are we going to meet up? I got a little something for you and Parisi—well, Aisling got it for me, because I don't have opposable thumbs—but I wasn't sure where to send it. You don't have to get me anything, if that's what you're worried about. Ash and Drake and the kids always go a little crazy, mostly because Drake is convinced his kids will hate him like he hated his batshit crazy dad unless he bends over backwards for them, which of course means they play him like a trombone. Man, you'd think a grown wyvern would have a backbone, but when it comes to the spawn, Drake's putty in their sticky fingers. And then Aisling tells the spawn it's better to give than to receive, so they dole out the goods, too. Aisling lets them fill my stocking, and they always go for the good duck jerky treats. Yum. But no complaints from me, since it means they're all generous when it comes to pressies. So, anyway, don't worry if you didn't get me anything. Not that I'd care anyway, because it's nice to have parents again, and that beats out everything under the tree.

ME

We're going to go to Paris after New Year's Day, so if you wanted to meet up there, I'm down for it. Just let me know where and when, and I'll talk to Aisling.

ME

Did you say how Mom was? Is her memory coming back? If you let me have your address, maybe I can swing by and remind her that she gave birth to me.

ME

Desi?

"Problems?" Aisling asked as she staggered past where I was lying on my new plush bed that looked like a miniature couch. It was her early Christmas present to me, and I had to say, I felt pretty regal in it. I mean, what beats a magnificent Newfie on a couch?

I watched her struggle with a bunch of wrapping paper, ribbon, assorted decorative pieces, and a wad of tissue paper. "Naw, just my dad being cryptic. I think that's his personality."

"Cryptic?" Two rolls of paper slid out of her grip. She swore in Magyar, which is about all she knows of the language. It's why she likes England over Hungary, I think. "What sort of cryptic? The sort of cryptic that means he's coming after us because we broke him and Parisi out of their respective underworlds? Or some other sort of cryptic that isn't going to have Drake demanding we return to Hungary? I really do not want to go back there. It's too cold."

I looked pointedly out of the window where a light dusting of snow had hit our house in London.

"Bah. Humbug," she said, trying to wave a hand, which just resulted in two more tubes of paper hitting the floor. "You know what I mean. What did he say?"

"He said it was his new phone." I pursed my lips. No new messages had come in. "I guess that's all he wanted me to know, although I did ask after my mom, and I figured he'd tell me how she was."

Aisling peered at my phone when I nosed it toward her.

"Huh. That is weird." Two sticky tape containers fell. We both ignored them. "I should probably warn Drake that Desi has resurfaced, since both your folks have been quiet for the last few months, but we're so close to Christmas, and the Sarkany is a few days away, and you know how uptight he gets when all the other wyverns are together. Let me know if your dad says anything else that might be problematic, OK?"

"Sure," I said, using a pencil in my teeth to type out a quick text. "But I'm not sure how much more problematic you get than the guy who created Abaddon."

ME

You there? Everything OK? You guys left in a bit of a dither, so I hope you're still not all doom and gloom and waging war against everyone.

"Oy," Ash said, and after I helped her gather up all the stuff she dropped, she went off to Drake's study to wrap presents. The spawn aren't allowed in there, so it's the only safe spot in the house to wrap.

She's going to wrap my stuff for you and Amelie, too, and send it over to Paris with one of the Green Dragons so you guys will have it before Christmas.

Two days later, we all trooped off to Soldy's house Dragonwood for the Sarkany. There was the usual bit of posturing with the wyverns when the couple of non-weyr tribes came around ('cause dragons are big on protocol, and also, they're very full of themselves, if you know what I mean), but soon everyone settled down to the big meeting.

I won't bore you with the details, mostly because I fell asleep after Ava—that's the youngest of Ash's spawn—made me drag her all around in a kid's wagon before the Sarkany. Normally, I wouldn't do that sort of thing, because what self-respecting demon allows himself to be turned into a horse, but Ava's not a bad spawn. She's pretty much an Aisling mini-me, which has Drake eyeing first her in obvious martrydom, then

Aisling, in a way that if I were a person, would have me giggling.

Kid also is a guardian, but I don't think either Aisling or Drake knows that yet. Bet her teen years are going to be awesome!

Anyhoo, I slept through most of the Sarkany, but woke up when a couple of the tribe masters got into it with each other.

Here's a who's who of...well...who. Eh. I can't make that sentence work right with voice-to-text, so moving on.

The wyvern and mate of the green dragons are Drake and Aisling.

The wyvern and mate of the silver dragons are Gabriel and May.

Baltic is wyvern of the light dragons, and Ysolde is his mate. There are also Pavel and his mate, Holland. They all live together at Dragonwood. Pavel is Baltic's right hand man and elite guard. He is the best because he lets me taste test anything that doesn't have ingredients bad for dogs. We love Pavel. Holland is also cool, but he mostly takes care of their kid, so I don't see him as much as I do Pavel.

The blue dragons are Bastian the wyvern, Phyllida his mate, and her scribe, Seawright Pendleton. Seawright goes where Phyllida goes, which means she gets to attend Sarkanies. The dragons don't like it, but since she doesn't really care about dragon politics, she mostly ignores everyone. The blue dragons are now technically the Song Tribe, but everyone still calls them blue dragons.

The black dragon wyvern is Kostya. Aoife is his mate. Kostya is the biggest drama queen you'll ever meet, and considering the dragons, that's saying a lot.

The red dragons are new since most of them were wiped out a few years ago. There's about twenty of them now, most of who rejoined the sept after Rowan took over as wyvern (they were in the lawless dragon tribes before that because they didn't like a seriously bad previous wyvern, Chuan Ren). Rowan's mate is Sophea, who smells really nice, and bought special dog treats for me when there was a Sarkany at her house last year. I had Aisling send her some chockies from me just so she'd know I appreciated the noms.

The indigo dragons are Constantine (wyvern)— who is also a drama queen, and who lives to pick fights with Kostya and Baltic, both of whom he has a beef with—and his mate, Bee, who is sister to Aoife and Rowan.

I haven't seen them in a while because they also had a kid, and I guess Constantine is a bit overly cautious. The best part of the Indigo sept is Gary, a disembodied head who rides around on a RC car. Gary's cool, although he does love to organize parties, and is always trying to talk Bee and Connie into having one.

There's a couple of new non-sept tribes that get invited to some of the Sarkanies. The Storm Tribe is headed up by Archer. His mate is Thaisa. Archer's twin brother is Hunter, who leads the Shadow Tribe. Both of them are sons of a nasty dragon by the name of Xavier. I won't go into what he's trying to do to everyone, but it involves a lot of death and sorrow, so you can imagine how many talks the dragons have over what to do with Xavier, etc.

Sheesh, that took a long time. I hope you're still awake. If not, I'm sure Amelie will continue reading when you're up again.

Anyway, I woke up when the shouting started.

"We wouldn't be in a situation where we had to deal with your homicidal father as well as Baltic's insane brother if you two hadn't dragged the weyr into the situation," Kostya was shouting when I got to my feet, had a good shake, sat down to consider what was going on.

Everyone was on their feet, the women mostly pulling the men out of what were clearly confrontational poses.

"It's your fault the weyr is at risk with Xavier targeting dragonkin. And for what? To turn us all into you?" Kostya snorted, outright snorted, which is never a good look, no matter how badass you are.

And to be honest, Kostya is badass, but still.

Aoife was plastered against his front, obviously keeping Kostya and Hunter apart.

For a minute, I thought my eyes were going wonky because although Hunter's arms were crossed, I could see his fingers moving, and they were shaping black symbols in the air.

I scooted over to where Aisling held Drake by one arm.

"Dude's drawing a pretty wicked spell," I told her sotto voce, but either my voce is off, or Hunter has really good hearing, because his head snapped around to shoot a glare at me that I felt right down to my toenails. "Also, Kostya may be a badass, but Hunter? Yeah, he's well beyond that vand into the realm of seriously worrisome."

Aisling, who had protested when I sat on her foot (it's my love language), stopped squawking and let go of Drake's arm to bend down and ask quietly, "Hunter is worrisome? He's casting a spell?"

"Yup. Watch his fingers."

We both looked at Hunter, who was ignoring Kostya continuing to bitch about Xavier in order to narrow his eyes at me.

"Dude," I said loudly. "It's not me who has a problem with you."

"Hrmph," he said, then to my intense pleasure, one of his fists shot out and he nailed Kostya on the jaw. "I tire of hearing you complain. Archer and I have told you all repeatedly that we will take care of the sire. You can take refuge with your sept until such time as we have rid the world of him."

"Oh!" Aoife yelled, and gave Hunter a shove on the chest. Normally, she's pretty quiet, so it took both of us by surprise when she went on the attack. "No one punches Kostya but me!"

Kostya, about to lay out Hunter (or try to), paused to glare at her.

She gave kind of a hiccupping laugh and said, "Sorry. No one punches Kostya, period."

"Thank you," he said in his stiff, outraged voice, the one that grates along the skin like a Victorian potato peeler. One that's been out in the rain for about a hundred years.

"I guess this is a sign that we'd better let everyone have their free-for-all before dinner," Ysolde said with a sigh, glancing at Aisling and May. "I was hoping we could wait until after everyone had eaten, so tempers would hopefully be smoothed over with good food and Baltic's expensive champagne—"

"Mate!" he said in his usual outraged tone, which makes Aisling and May giggle. They did so now as Ysolde turned a bland expression on Baltic.

"We are the senior dragons," she pointed out. "It is our duty to treat the rest of the weyr—and those ouroboros tribes that are weyr-adjacent—with appropriate hospitality, and that means your good Bolly is making a showing. You wouldn't want the other wyverns thinking we're cheap, would you?"

"Senior dragons? Both of you are less than five years old, technically," Drake said, a little curl of smoke coming out of his nose as he glared at Constantine. I gathered I'd missed some sort of argument between them. "But by all means, if you wish to name yourselves as the highest of high, do so."

"We are senior because we both remember very well when you were a puling little babe," Ysolde said in the silky smooth voice that had a smile curling the corners of Baltic's mouth. Like the mates, he knew what was coming. "The puling didn't stop when you were an adult, did it, Drake Fekete? I distinctly recall a time at the start of the sixteenth century when your wyvern had to seek Baltic's help to break you out of a French prison."

"You were in prison?" Aisling asked Drake, who by now was wearing an expression that was part martyrdom, and part regret.

He made an abbreviated gesture of dismissal, and moved his glare over to Ysolde, who was standing with her arm around Baltic, leaning into him. I won't say Baltic looked happy, because he never looked happy, but enjoyment lit his eyes as Drake tried to smooth over his past.

"It was just a minor situation, one quickly resolved, and of no importance," he said, and after another twist of smoke emerged from his nose, told Hunter, "The weyr has stated its intention to aid in the locating and imprisonment or destruction of Xavier, as you well know, so threatening Kostya will lead to no productive acts."

Aisling leaned around him to ask Ysolde, "Why was Drake in prison?"

"He was shtupping Henry IV's queen," Ysolde answered blithely, her smile warm and genuine, and which always made me feel toasty. Mostly because I love it when she goes after Drake. She knows the best gossip!

"And a good number of her ladies in waiting," Baltic added, his lips twitching a couple of times as Drake shot him an absolutely outraged look. "There was a rumor he seduced some of the king's courtiers, and even had a shot at the king, as well."

Aisling looked startled. "I didn't know you were into men as well as women."

"I'm not!" Drake fired off another glare at Ysolde and Baltic, and blatantly ignored the subdued laughter from everyone else present as he dragged Aisling backward to have a quiet discussion.

"Are we having fisticuffs or not?" Baltic asked Ysolde. "If not, I have other things to do."

"Fisticuffs?" Charity asked. Did I mention her? She's the mate of the Big Daddy, the First Dragon, the demigod who started the whole race, and who is the ancestor of every dragon who ever was, and ever will be. He likes to say that, so I thought I'd repeat it for you. "You guys fight at your get-togethers?"

"Just the men," May said as she helped Gabriel get out of a really pretty black suit coat that was embroidered with silver dragons. "We let them go ham on each other when they get a bit testy."

"Reasonable ham, that is. Nothing lethal. We've found it relieves the tensions, and makes everyone more agreeable," Aisling said to the group before turning to Drake and adding, "We're going to have a talk later about your time in France."

"I hope you're satisfied," Drake told Ysolde grumpily, but wasted no time in taking off his suit coat, tie, and shirt.

The other wyverns and tribe masters took one look at his bare chest, and the shirts went a-flying.

"I'm still not sure what this is all about," Thaisa complained as we followed the others when Ysolde told the men she and Pavel had set up a special pen for the brawl, and they headed out the door to a small paddock at the back of the house. The snow had melted the day before, and it was well above freezing, but still chilly enough to make me appreciate my magnificent fluff.

"Whoa. Festive!" I said when we got there. Although it was just a standard pen with a small walk in shed for Ysolde's youngest son's pony, Ysolde had festooned the railings with lit garlands and blow up ornaments. Santa and elf balloons were tied along the top rail, and in the center of the pen, a large new metal garbage bin was filled with what looked like six foot tall candy canes.

"Holy moly, you really went all out for this!" Aisling said as she moved over to a row of chairs that had been set up for spectators.

I gave Ysolde a bump on the leg. She looked down. "You host the best parties. Thanks for thinking of me," I said, and gave her a little rub with my head. She smiled, and once again I felt all warm, and happily settled down on the dog bed she'd set up with the chairs.

"This is amazing!" May said as the men, with odd looks at the decorations, proceeded into the round pen. "I can't believe you went to all this trouble. Are those... jousting tools?"

"Foam candy canes," Ysolde said, picking up a small bullhorn. "I found them online. I figured the boys might want a change from punching each other, and can fight with them, instead."

Kostya plucked one from the bin, and waggled it around for a few seconds, before saying, "They're impractical. They're too soft to do any damage to Constantine."

"The same could be said about you," Connie snapped back, making Bee choke with laughter.

Kostya snarled something rude in Zilant (the dragons' native tongue before everyone switched to English), and slammed the foam candy cane back into the bin.

"You boys know the rules," Ysolde said through the bullhorn, making Phyllida, who was standing next to her quietly explaining to Seawright what was going on, jump a good two feet straight up. "Fists or foam candy canes only. No dragon form. No fire. No going for the noogies, for obvious reasons. If you hurt yourself seriously, Gabriel will apply his magic spit to heal you."

Gabriel cocked an eyebrow when Kostya made gagging noises.

"I have a bounty for the person who breaks Kostya's collarbone first," Baltic announced. "A full case of 1921 Dragon's Blood."

Ysolde, who had turned to address her housekeeper as the latter rolled out a trolley of drinks and nibblies, whipped around to say through the bullhorn, "By the rood, man, you're the host! You don't set bounties on your guests being harmed! There will be no payment to anyone for hurting Kostya."

"They can try, but they won't succeed!" the man himself said with a few indignant snorts directed towards Baltic.

Ysolde thought for a moment, then added, "You can beat him silly with the candy canes, though. If you can take him down with those, then you can have Baltic's wine."

"Ysolde!" Kostya roared, looking outraged as per normal.

Baltic smiled, and flexed his fingers.

"Oooh. Canapes for the ass-kicking is setting a new standard," Aisling said as she and Aoife hovered over the snacks. "No one will ever be able to touch you for your Sarkany hosting after this. Are those stuffed mushroom caps?"

"We have enough here to do teams," Drake said, and immediately, he and Kostya buddied up, as did the dragon hunter twins, Archer and Hunter.

Bastian and Baltic retreated to one side of the pen, Bastian gesticulating with one of the foam candy canes as he and Baltic clearly made plans. Gabriel wore a close approximation to Drake's martyred expression when Constantine claimed him as a teammate, while Rowan and Feodorit (he's the master of the Fire Tribe who recently joined up to battle Xavier) each took a candy cane, and gestured toward Kostya as they consulted.

"Yes, and the ones on the tray that Esmerelda is bringing out now has dog-safe ingredients. No onions, garlic, or any of the other nasties that Pavel researched."

"I'm not sure...you're certain they won't get hurt?" Sophea, Rowan's mate, asked. I liked her because she had a soft voice, and found the itchy spot behind my left ear. "Rowan is new to being a dragon, after all."

"That's why we limit them to mortal fighting only. They can heal themselves of minor hurts," Aisling told her as she moaned softly when popping a samosa into her mouth.

Sophea didn't look any too convinced, but since the rest of the mates were mostly focused on the eats, she evidently decided not to voice any more concerns.

Ysolde lifted the bullhorn again. "Ready? You have ten minutes. And...go!"

"You guys really are the best," I said around a mouthful of sharp cheddar cheese that Aisling had given me. Ysolde handed out glasses of Baltic's expensive champagne while various battle cries filled the air as the dragons all surged forward from their respective areas.

Aisling filled me a plate from the dog-safe food, which made me determined to get Soldy and Pavel a better present next year. This year I was limited to what Aisling wanted, but since she'd given me my own credit card, I was free to go wild.

"So they just beat each other—hey! Ysolde said no hitting on the groin! Rowan and I haven't even talked about kids yet, although evidently we have to have at least one in order to make the First Dragon happy," Sophea said loudly, glaring at Gabriel and Constantine when they jumped team Rowan and Feo, both of whom went down with a defensive flurry of foam candy canes.

Everyone turned to look at Charity, who had a mouth full of herbed goat cheese, and was dipping a bit of flatbread into a smoked eggplant dip. She froze for a second, then gave a half shrug and continued chewing. "I'm not sure what you expect me to say, but if you don't want children, I can mention that to the First Dragon."

"We're not saying that," Sophea protested, setting a piece of smoked salmon tart on a plate before hesitating over the chimichurri meatballs. I made a face at the latter since it was on the verboten table, but I figured I wouldn't complain. It was the holidays, after all, and Ysolde did a Sarkany right. "We just haven't talked overly much about it yet. Someday, but not right now. We both still feel like we're learning how to dragon properly. These meatballs look enticing. How spicy are they?"

"Hotter than what I'd like, but Baltic and Pavel overrode my preference. Try one of these shrimp cakes, instead. They have roasted garlic, and are to die for."

All the mates zoomed in on the platter holding the shrimp cakes.

I'll skip over the next ten minutes, because to be honest, I was fully involved in eating some cheesy bread, crostini with salmon, and ham and cheese sliders, but by the time all the mates were moaning almost nonstop over the noms, the timer on Aisling's phone went off, and all the men collapsed to the ground.

Immediately, the complaining started.

"It is not broken," Kostya said through his teeth when Aoife helped him limp over to the chairs. Ysolde had brought out the dragon's blood wine, which the men tended to use as a pick-me-up after they beat each other to a pulp. "I don't know why you think it is. My collarbone is perfectly solid. It doesn't break at a whim."

"Raise your left arm," Aoife told him, accepting a paper cup of wine and holding it just out of his reach.

Kostya started to move his arm, grimaced, swore under his breath, and glared at Aoife until she handed him the wine.

"You're just lucky you heal fast," she said before taking up a couple of wet wipes and dabbing at the blood on his face.

"Looks like you lost a tooth. I thought that was your brother's schtick," I told him.

He set my tail on fire, but I was ready for it, and plopped down on his foot to put it out.

"Jim, stop taunting Kostya. Drake, it's clearly dislocated, so stop trying to put your shirt on. Gabriel? Can we have a shoulder consult? Here, sweetie, drink this. Sorry. Use your other hand to take...oh. I see. Gabriel, we need a hand intervention, too. I don't think Drake's finger is suppose to bend sideways like that."

"It'll be a minute," May called from where she was squatting next to Gabriel. He was slumped over, rubbing his knee. "He's just trying to get his knee working again so he can walk. I don't know which of you kicked him on it, but you are due some seriously bad juju for taking out the healer."

"It was Hunter," Archer said. He didn't look too bad, just had a couple of big gashes on his face, and a clear footprint on his chest, but appeared to be sitting pretty comfortably. His mate made distressed sounds as she dabbed at the cuts, and I could hear her muttering in an old Eastern European language about men and their misguided egos. "But he was aiming for the spirit. Gabriel got in the way."

"My apologies," Hunter moaned. He was lying on the ground, and Ysolde and Aisling took turns tending to him. "I'll aim better next time. Assuming I survive. I think my internal organs have imploded."

"Bah," Ysolde said, waving off his complaint before taking up more wine. "Thaisa says you guys are some sort of dragon superheroes, so I'm sure you'll be fine. Oh, Gabriel. Ow. Did you hurt yourself? Let's get you back into your chair, and I'll give you two glasses of dragon's blood."

A pathetic, "Mate!" emerged from Baltic's bloody lips.

"Yes, my wounded hero, I'm coming. Just keep that ice pack on your lip and cheek. Did everyone who needs it get their wine?" she asked, holding up a bottle and glancing around.

"I'm dead," Constantine said. He was flat out on my dog bed, moaning whenever Bee wiped at a wound.

"Yes, but you're charming anyway," Bee told him, kissing him on a non-bloody part of his face. "And you wielded your candy cane well."

"I walloped my godson with it repeatedly," Connie said proudly, one very swollen eye opening a crack as he smiled at Bee. She winced at the fact that he was obviously missing his two front teeth.

"I'll give you the name of our dentist in Paris," Aisling told Bee as she went to fetch Drake a few of the softer treats. "He's done a wonderful job replacing all the teeth Drake's lost over the years."

Drake stiffened, obviously ran his tongue around his mouth, then slumped. "I'll need an appointment as well."

"Oh, no, really? You're not going to have any of your own teeth left if you keep going like this," Aisling said, and hurried back to soothe him.

"I'd rather have fake teeth than a feeble collarbone," Bastian announced. He listed in his chair, but looked happy as Phyllida fed him bits of ricotta and roasted grapes.

"My collarbone is not—ow! Aoife!" Kostya almost roared when Aoife, with a practiced hand, accepted the large roll of elastic bandage that Pavel was passing out to anyone who needed them, and bound Kostya's left arm to his chest.

"Stop fighting me, and let me strap your arm down so your collarbone can mend. There. Now, don't move. Do you want some of the roasted shrimp cocktail, or the spicy steak bits?"

"Dragons like meat," he said in his patented Kostya Grumpy Voice, but he was clearly happy when Aoife brought him both.

It took another forty minutes before everyone was fed, healed up enough that they could move without groaning (or in Kostya's case, bitching about everyone trying to break his bones for a case of champagne), and then after the wine was handed over to Bastian as winner of the collarbone award, everyone went in for the big dinner.

Almost three hours later, the dragons filed out and said their goodbyes.

"Another successful Sarkany," I told Aisling as I flopped onto the floor of Drake's vintage Rolls. "Are we stopping for a snack on the way home? It's at least two hours before we get to London and my superb form needs sustenance. I bet there's a burger place that's open. I could really go for a burger right now."

Aisling nudged me with her toe. "You have eaten enough food for three Newfies, and don't even think of giving me the look I know you're warming up, because it's only a few days until Christmas, and if you want Santa to give you that membership to the doggy aquatic therapy place, you'd better not be any trouble."

"Trouble?" I said, gasping. "Me? Are you insane? I am never any trouble. Plus, Newfies are water dogs, and the therapy place has people who will swim with you, and they have fun games and things."

"Mmmhmm." Aisling snuggled into Drake, who looked pretty pleased despite occasionally screwing up his face as he obviously felt the spot where one of his teeth had been. "I'm glad the Sarkany is over, though. Now we can all relax, and enjoy the peace of the holidays."

My phone pinged as I was trying to figure out a nice way to tell her that where her spawn were concerned, there was no such thing as peace, but in the spirit of the season, I didn't.

Then I got a look at my phone.

DESISLAV
Effrijim
DESISLAV
Prepare yourself.
DESISLAV
It has begun.

VAMPIRE IN A PEAR TREE
A RAVENFALL NOVELLA

ONE
OWAIN

"And a merry fucking Christmas to you, you ungrateful whelp!"

Owain ap Aidan eyed his mother and wondered what bee had gotten up her bustle. All he'd done was to wish her a happy holiday.

"No matcha latte available at the local shop?" he asked, taking a seat in the sitting room of an expensive house in the middle of an exclusive area in London, mindful of the raven perched on his shoulder.

"No, and don't think the manager didn't hear about his fundamental failure when it came to the bare minimum of organizational responsibilities demanded by his position. How hard can it be to keep suitable amounts of matcha powder in stock? Mortals these days really grind my gears," she said, pacing across the somewhat dark room, one hand gesturing sharply as she spoke.

"Angharad—" he started to say, one eye on the street beyond the window. It was supposed to snow later that day, and he wanted to get this audience with his mother over quickly.

The rest of the unspoken sentence dried up when she whirled around, her long blonde hair whipping out in a manner that had him involuntarily flinching backward, causing Orla to squawk a protest when her tail feathers were squished.

"You idiot! Have a little consideration for my feathers! You're so careless with me! If you keep treating me this way, I'll leave you!"

"Promises, promises," he murmured under his breath, shooting a warning glare at the raven when she made a movement like she was about to poop on his shoulder.

"I've told you to stop using that name! It's my … what do people call it? … dead name." His mother donned an expression that Owain assumed was her version of being nobly martyred. He knew she understood Orla's raucous caws as well as he did, but was evidently not offended by the bird's comments toward him.

"Angharad ferch Cailitin is a dead name?" He wondered what she was up to by denying her identity. "I admit the *ferch Cailitin* part is not commonly used these days, but you could simply adopt Cailitin as your surname."

She squared her shoulders, causing Orla to take a step back and flap her wings in obvious warning. "I will do no such thing. For one, I wouldn't dream of honoring that fatheaded druid who calls himself my father by using his name as my surname, and for another, you've been in the mortal world for almost a year now—surely you must know that it's highly improper for you to call me by a name I don't want."

"Would you prefer Morrigan?" he asked, throwing caution to the wind. The meetings with his mother were growing increasingly tense due to her stubbornness.

She came perilously close to spitting words out at him, jabbing a finger painfully into his chest. "Are you deliberately trying to enrage me? Do you want me to smite you and that moldy bird on the spot? You will *not* use my dead names!"

He didn't think it was possible for a raven to gasp in outrage, but Orla managed it before cawing, "I am not moldy!"

"You are not transgender that I know of," he told his mother.

"I am the most feared hedge witch in all of Dalriada!" Orla glared at the woman before them.

"In addition to which, I don't think simply calling yourself by a new name is the same as someone who is no longer comfortable with their birth name for reasons of misgendering." He ignored Orla's comments in order to focus on hurrying his mother along. He had places to be, and elusive dragons to find.

Orla ruffled up her feathers and stomped her feet on his shoulder. "My cousin was wed to a friend of a groom of one of the stewards to a great king!"

"Pah," his mother said, waving away his explanation. "I took the name Jericho when I was with the Court of Divine Blood. You can call me Jerry if you want to keep up with the times. That point aside, no one has called me the Morrigan in centuries. Not since my father dragged us from Ireland to Wales. Besides, the Morrigna is no more."

He frowned. What was this? "It's not? I thought the Morrigna was made up of three Morrigans, aka you and two of your four sisters?"

"Yes, well …" She gave a little cough. "It so happens that one of those sisters is no more, so technically, the Morrigna doesn't exist."

"Which sister?" he asked, noting the way she refused to meet his gaze.

"She offed her own sister. Her own sister!" Orla gave an avian snort. "I don't know why you act surprised. You know how your mother is!"

"Ozy. She died last year, right before you came out of the Hour." His mother flicked a gaze toward Orla. "And I am the daughter of a druid, bird. Remember that when you think to speak ill of me!"

"Shite," Orla swore under her breath, scooting over closer to his ear. "Can all your family understand me?"

"Yes." He thought of asking what had happened to his aunt, but decided he really didn't want to get involved in his mother's latest scheme. Those seldom ended well for anyone. "I'm sorry to hear about the death of Ozymandra. As regards your choice of names, I'm happy to call you Jericho, or whatever name you like, so long as you get to the point of this meeting. I am working hard to find a solution to the problem at hand."

"Bah," she said, pacing to an elaborately decorated Christmas tree at the window before turning back. "You'll never get that curse lifted. Not without my help, and you won't have that until you return my powers to me."

"The very same powers that are keeping me sane?" He gave an abrupt shake of his head. "You've gotten along fine without them for almost two millennia. Not to mention that you must have taken back that which you gave to Cadell."

She gave a derisive snort. "Of course I took it back from that idiot. I never should have bestowed him with it, but I was misled by you boys until I fell into your plans. Well, no more! That fool Cernunnos has taken over as head of the Celtic Pantheon, and instigated a new rule that prohibits membership from those who don't possess all their powers. I refuse to be treated in such a cavalier manner! I am a Morrigan!"

"You just said you didn't like that name—" Owain pointed out her hypocrisy even as Orla gave a burst of laughter that emerged as a rusty caw.

"I am the goddess of war and fate, daughter of the druid Cailitin, and sister to twenty-seven brothers!" Jericho said even louder, drowning him out.

Owain, knowing well what was coming, and waiting for the count of three that his mother always took before reciting her greatest life moments, said in perfect synchronicity with her, "I tested the courage of kings, and would withhold my blessing should they not sufficiently impress me!"

"I heard that she used to bed the kings, and the ones who didn't please her were left without her grace on the battlefield. I can't imagine being so callous," Orla said with a pointed sniff.

"Says the woman who tried to decapitate me," he told the bird, unable to resist responding to her unwarranted scorn.

"What?" Jericho, who had been going on about how important she, her sisters, and the brothers who made up Clan Cailitin were to the rulers of early Irish history, missed Orla's comment.

He gestured away the question. "It's just Orla being her usual self. Regardless of your importance, I think you'll survive the few months it will take me to find someone who can break the curse."

"Usual self? Usual self!" Orla turned her head so one beady yellow eye stared balefully at him. "My usual self is a comely maiden with the ability to beguile men and make the rowan bloom. And the sooner you hurry up your pitiful attempts to rid yourself of that curse, the sooner you can return me to my natural state, and I can go back to Ireland where I belong."

"They're *my* powers!" Jericho raged, slapping her hands down onto a small chess table in front of him. "I never intended for you and your brothers to keep them! They were supposed to help you and Rhain take down those pesky demon lords. That's all! Now that you've escaped from the Hour where your brothers are still being held captive, you can bloody well give back what is mine. If for no other reason than as penance for abandoning your beloved brothers by thinking only of yourself and your selfish needs."

"I doubt if anyone who had their soul ripped out while the curse of bloodlust was placed upon them would view having said curse removed as selfish, but this is an old argument, and a false one at that. I didn't escape the Seventh Hour; I was ejected from it without warning. As for my *beloved* brothers—the last time I saw Rhain, he lopped off one of my arms and would have gelded me if Rhys hadn't stopped him." He flexed his left arm, the memory of the month it took for a mage to reattach the severed arm still a cause of irritation. "I don't know what Cadell did during that time, since I assume he was re-imprisoned in the Hour when I was expulsed."

"*Tch,*" Jericho said, storming past him only to spin on her heel and return. "He was almost as useless out in the mortal world as you are."

He stood up, having caught the slight movement of white out of his peripheral vision. "I've sworn to return the power you bestowed upon me as soon as I break the curse, so if that's all you want to say to me, I'll be on my way. I have a lead on a charmer who might be able to help, but she's not easy to contact."

"A charmer?" Jericho made a noise of dismissal. "I told you at the time those demon lords cursed you boys that no mere charmer could break it."

"Which is why I'm trying to contact a charmer who is a dragon's mate," Owain answered, picking up the fedora he had taken to wearing in the daylight. While he didn't suffer the same effects of the bloodlust curse that had resulted in modern-day Dark Ones, being out in daylight wasn't overly comfortable. "She has more abilities than a normal charmer. Unfortunately, she's being particularly difficult to find, and I may end up resorting to a thief taker to find her."

"A what?" Jericho asked, her frown prodigious. Owain watched her with a wariness born of long familiarity with both his mother's mood swings and the power she still commanded despite bestowing much of it on himself and his brothers.

"Thief taker. Someone who will find a person being sought, in this case, the dragon charmer."

"Oh, them." She gave a roll of her eyes as she strode across the room again, ignoring him standing near the door. "I don't know why you refuse to listen to me about this—no charmer is going to be able to break the curse, dragon-born or otherwise. Not now that Desislav is out in the mortal world again."

He had reached for the doorknob when she spoke, but he froze as her words percolated through the desire to leave, his fingers a scant inch from the glass doorknob. Feeling as if he were as frozen as the ground outside, he asked, "You—he's out? How can that be? He was in the Thirteenth Hour. No one can escape from there."

Jericho shrugged and strode past him, her hands moving in a way that had him wondering if she was about to cast a spell. "I don't know how he got out, but Vera says a fury is hunting for the blood moon, and has offered some big reward for it."

Owain could swear he turned into a man-sized block of ice. A *livid* block of ice. "The blood moon is still in existence? It's being hunted by others? Who?"

"Vera told me there were mercenaries popping up all over the place to try to find it and claim the reward." She straightened up a vase filled with holly, sliding him a look that had warning bells sounding in his head.

He thought seriously about hyperventilating, but decided it was beneath him. He'd wait until he returned to his temporary lodgings before he gave in to the panic attack that was threatening to swamp him. "The blood moon was destroyed," he said in a voice that rivaled Orla's roughest croak.

"So we thought, but evidently it isn't. Regardless, you see why I need to be back on the Celtic Pantheon. If I had my full complement of powers, then that annoying Cernunnos couldn't ban me from rejoining, and I could help you all, my most beloved sons."

Owain wasn't at all fooled by the sudden syrupy tone of his mother's words. "If what Badb said is true—"

"Vera," Jericho interrupted him. "Badb calls herself Vera now. You really need to get with the times, Owain. Even Cadell gave himself a modern name, although it was foolish and I don't remember what it was."

"The last thing I need is the blood moon falling into Desi's hands. He'll throw me back into the Hour again!" Fury roared to life within him. "I must find it before anyone else. It's the only way I can ensure our freedom."

"Yes, yes, but you see that I can help you if I have my power back." Jericho had donned her most persuasive of attitudes, patting him on the arm as her black gaze burned deep into the spot where his soul once resided.

"How?" he asked, too shaken to phrase the question nicely. "What can you do? You can't lift the curse. You couldn't when Desi and the two other demon princes placed the bloodlust upon us, and it's had time to strengthen over the millennia."

"No, of course I can't remove the curse, but I can do other things." Her look turned coy as she absently moved a particularly hideous Santa figurine. "I can get your brothers out, for one."

He thought about it for a few moments, really thought about it. "You may believe me to be unfeeling when it comes to them, but Rhain harbors too much rage to be anything but a danger to the mortal world, and should not be released. Rhys … Rhys is Rhys. I have no idea what he's thinking. I never have, but he has never been fond of mortals. Cadell is evidently not a threat, but regardless, until I can have the curse lifted, it's better if they stay where they are."

"You refuse my request, then?" Jericho said, her voice as soft as the wind as she faced him, but instantly, Owain was on his guard.

"Goddess! She's going to smite us on the spot! Run! We must escape! You can't end my curse until your own is broken, and there's no way you can do that if you're dead!" Orla flapped her wings in warning, making him squint to keep her feathers from his eyes.

"I will return what was given to me as soon as the curse is broken," he said, anger rising at the idea of Desislav the Destroyer being once again in possession of the blood moon.

Bitterness mingled with regret. Why his brothers and he had thought destroying Abaddon was a good way to save mortals was now beyond him. He'd had almost two millennia to realize the sheer folly of their plan.

It didn't mean he was ready to martyr himself by imprisonment in the Hour, however.

There was no doubt that Desi in possession of the blood moon was a direct threat, one he would move the stars in the sky to avoid.

"Very well," his mother said, and, before Owain could say another word, threw her hands wide, the spell she'd been weaving slamming him in the face and sending him reeling backward into darkness, her words following him into its inky depths. "You want me to be part of the Morrigna again? Far be it from me to deny my child at Christmas. I will summon my sisters, and with their help, I will extract from you what is mine."

TWO
BERRY

"The Respectful Order of Knockers, Coblyns, and Bluecaps can bite my shiny pink ass. The nerve of them kicking me out over nothing! And so close to Christmas! I tell you, Savian, it's all politics with the knockers now. You put so much as one toe out of what they consider a reasonable line, and boom! You're booted out into the cold, hard, unemployed world. It doesn't matter how many decades you've devoted to them, oh no, you take a stand to protect Gaia, and they have the hissy fit to end all hissy fits. I won't even repeat the things they said about me, but you can rest assured that it was all bull." I panted a little at the end of the rant, but that was mostly because I'd worked myself into a rage during the walk to my cousin's house.

Savian, who sat in a wheelchair at the front door of his house in a London suburb, blinked at me a couple of times before he gave me a bright smile. "Hullo, Berry. I suppose you shouldn't have helped with the downfall of that fracking company if it was going to get you fired."

"Fracking is bad," I reminded him, entering the house when he wheeled backward and gestured me in, careful to avoid his legs, both in casts from the knees down. "It's harmful to the earth, and what is a knocker if not a being who devotes her life to protecting said earth. How are you feeling? You have color back in your face, so Maura must be taking good care of you."

"She is, I have, and better, thank you. Still can't take a shower, but Maura has been very inventive in helping me bathe." His eyebrows waggled even as he grinned before spinning around and preceding me into a sunny sitting room that faced a narrow, but tidy, back garden. "She and the kids are off seeing her mum, but they'll be back by dinnertime, if you'd like to stay."

"Wish I could, but I have to try to find someone who'll take on my unemployed self. If you have any ideas, I'd love to hear them, because I can't even get an interview."

"As a matter of fact—oh, ta. No milk, and one sugar, please. As a matter of fact, I might have something you could do, although it would require you to pass a background check with the Committee." He accepted the cup of tea that I'd poured him when I realized his wife, Maura, a lovely dragon with a wicked sense of humor, had set an electric kettle and tea makings on a side table within his reach.

I paused in the act of pouring myself a cup, studying his face. Although Savian had been born mortal, he was now a dragon's mate and, as such, had stopped aging. His long, very English face had a few more lines than I remembered the last time I'd seen him, but he looked much the same.

Spurred by a sudden rush of emotions, I gave his arm a squeeze and said, "I'm so glad you found Maura. Life with her and the kids obviously suits you. You look happy despite two obliterated legs. Speaking of that, did they ever find the troll who threw you onto the train tracks?"

He gave a little shudder, and took a sip of tea before answering. "Yes, although since there were no cameras around that section of the track, it's my word against his. Luckily, I'm healing two shattered legs faster than a mortal, so I should be mobile in a few more days. And I agree with the sentiment that Maura and the sprogs make my life worth living. But we're here to talk about you. It's why I invited you around."

"And here I was hoping you wanted to feed me so I wouldn't expire of starvation," I said with a wry smile, one that acknowledged there was little chance my substantial self would fade away anytime soon. "How are the kids? The baby is almost a year, yes?"

We spent a good ten minutes talking about his life pre–troll attack, and I admired many photos of his two daughters and one son, as well as a smiling Maura.

"Back to what you said—I'm happy to feed you, but really, I wanted you here for two reasons: one was to tell you about the job opportunity, and the other was to share our good news. I should wait for Maura to be here, but I don't think she'll mind me spilling it to you."

"You're having another baby?" I asked, surprised but pleased for them. Savian had been a well-known ladies' man for most of his life, but once he met Maura, he turned into an admirable husband and father.

"No, I think we're done there. Although … no. We're good with three. Our news is that we're about to become official dragons." He beamed with obvious pleasure.

"I thought Maura was a dragon already. Is it because her mom is human that she isn't considered one?" I asked, confused.

"No, not at all. In fact, quite the opposite—she could be a wyvern if she wanted," he answered, offering me a box of cookies. I picked out one, fighting to keep from stuffing it in my face. "And since I assume that look of confusion means you don't know what a wyvern is, they are the leaders of the various dragon groups called septs. We've accepted the offer made by the wyvern of the red sept to formally become members. Maura's father was a red dragon, you see, so it makes sense for us to join the sept now that it's been re-formed."

"Congrats to all of you. Will that mean any changes for you working as a thief taker?"

"As I'm freelance, not a one," he said, offering me the biscuit tin again, winking when I hesitated. "Go ahead. You've got that look in your eyes that says you'd eat roast behemoth if you had the chance."

I limited my second dip into the cookies to just two more, giving him a grateful glance. "I may not look like I've been on a tight budget, but I assure you I am, so thank you for this treat. What job do you think I would be able to get for the Committee?"

"My old job, as a matter of fact," he said, shifting his legs. I grabbed a couple of small pillows he had strained to reach, and propped them under his legs so they were at a more comfortable angle. "I left off being an official thief taker for the L'au-dela seven years ago, and although they've had a few people fill the role, no one's stuck to it for more than a half year. You have the heritage, the brains, and a brilliant cousin who will impart to you all of his knowledge about the ways of tracking, so I have no doubt you'd be perfect for the job."

"A thief taker," I said slowly, musing over the idea. Our grandfather had been a well-known thief taker, and although my side of the family had never followed that path—my father was a knocker, and passed that on down to me—Savian had a point. I did have tracking in my blood. "Hmm. It's not a bad idea, so long as you let me know best practices."

"I thought you'd like it," he said, his smile both warm and somewhat smug as he leaned back in his chair. "The application is online. I'm happy to help you fill it out, if you'd like."

I jumped on the offer, and spent the rest of the afternoon with him. By the time Maura and the kids returned, I'd filled out the application, uploaded my CV, washed the tea things, and, under Savian's supervision, whipped up two shepherd's pies and a batch of my grandmother's Moravian spice cookies. Dinner was a bit chaotic, but as I genuinely liked Maura and the children, I returned home to my dark room with a full stomach, a container of leftover dinner, and, more important, hope for my future.

Five days later, after a trip to Paris to meet with Savian's grandfather-in-law (the man who basically ran the European Otherworld) Dr. Kostich, I was granted the title of provisional thief taker of the L'au-dela.

Twelve hours after I returned to London clutching a card naming me as an employee of the Committee, I got a phone call.

"I need a thief taker in London," a woman said without a greeting. "You're the only one who is in town. How quickly can you find my son?"

"I don't know," I said, a bit confused. "Why don't you start by telling me how old he is? Also, the mortal police are very good at tracking lost children, so I'd recommend you talk to them, too—"

"I don't know the exact year Owain was born, because we didn't number things at that time, but it was the year we had an eclipse. I distinctly remember the mortals believing the world had come to an end."

I pursed my lips at her answer, and pulled out a small notebook and pen to take down relevant information. "OK. I'm glad it's not a missing child we're looking for. Can I get your name for my records, please? And also, tell me about your son."

"I'm Jericho Taf, although you may call me Jerry. My eldest son's name is Owain, which, since it's pronounced 'Owen,' is modern enough, I suppose, although I pointed out to him that we've all taken other names to fit in. All but my sister Ozymandra, and she insisted on keeping her name despite me warning her that she would never pass as mortal if she did. But she's dead now, so I suppose it's a moot point."

"I'm so sorry," I murmured, wondering about this potential client. Was she just talkative, or a bit scatty? It was hard to tell at this point.

"Eh. It's not the tragedy you imagine, although I did think Cadell could have dealt with her without having a demon lop off her head, but there you are."

I stared in growing horror at the ugly carpet of my rented room. "Someone hired a demon to kill your sister? Was it your son?"

"Yes. Cadell, although he uses another name now. Devon? Dermott? Something along those lines."

I was silent for almost half a minute before I could interrupt her stream of consciousness. "I'm sure names are important, but right now I'd like to gather some information about your son. Er ... the one you're looking for, not the demon-hiring one."

"Owain was ... staying with me for a bit." There was an odd note to her voice that I couldn't pinpoint, but I had a feeling it was anger. "He left without me knowing, he and that mangy bird he insists on keeping. I want you to find him."

"Not that I wish to pry, but is there a reason why your son can't be out on his own?" I asked, mindful of the instruction I'd been receiving from Savian to get me up to speed. "That is to say, is he mentally at risk if he was out in the mortal world?"

Her voice was filled with irritation. "His mind is all there. Such as it is. No, you need to find him because he has something of mine, and I want it back."

I waited for her to mention whatever it was he had taken, but she hummed "Last Christmas" softly to herself.

"OK. Can you send me a picture of him? And what was his last known location?"

"A photo? I don't think I have one. He's been in the Hour until a year ago, and I certainly haven't taken a photo of him. But he's very distinctive looking. He takes after his father that way. He's very tall, and has what the ladies call salt-and-pepper hair, which unfortunately he wears in a hip-hop style."

Hip-hop style? I wondered what that was.

"He has pale gray eyes with a thick black ring around the colored part. What do they call it?"

"Iris?" I asked, making notes.

"Yes. He's also very handsome. That he gets from my side of the family. My father—benighted as he was—was very handsome. It's why he had so many women after my mother died. I have twenty-seven brothers, and four sisters. Or I did have. Now there are three of my sisters remaining. Owain left sometime in the last couple of hours. I had to leave the house to procure an item from a mage, and when I returned, he had escaped."

"Escaped?" I repeated, my sense of unease growing. What the hell was going on with this woman? And did I want to get mixed up with whatever it was?

I glanced around the small, somewhat damp, and completely depressing room, and shook my head at my own thoughts. I didn't have a choice. A job was a job was a job.

"Left," she corrected. "Him and the bird. Did I mention her? She's a raven—my family has an affinity with them—but one of her wings doesn't work right, so she's always attached to Owain in some way or other. Truly, you don't have to worry about her. She's nothing but trouble, so I won't be bothered if you can't find her. It's Owain that matters."

I bit back both the comment that I didn't tolerate people who abused animals, including abandonment, and the fact that as a knocker, I also had the ability to talk to birds, and instead made a note that the mysterious Owain had a bird with him.

"How quickly can you find him?" Jerry asked.

"I don't quite know until I get out there and see what sort of a trail he left," I said, then felt obligated to add, "As the Committee exchange probably told you, I am a provisional thief taker, so I don't have a lot of practice tracking, although it is in my heritage, and my cousin has been guiding me. He's quite a well-known thief taker. Can you tell me what elemental class, if any, your son belongs to?"

"He's a thane," she said abruptly. "All my sons are thanes, although that is part of the present situation with Owain."

I had Google up and was searching before she finished. "Your sons are kings?" I asked, a bit overwhelmed at the thought of such a daunting first job.

"No, they're thanes. They are the creators of the race of Dark Ones, although they didn't know at the time that would be the result of the curse. And of course, all of them had sons, and the sins of the fathers passed to the sons, which is why the Dark Ones are the way they are. True, they went through some interim stage where they exploded all the time, but they worked past that with some mortal blood mixed into their gene pool."

"Hold up," I said, still staring at nothing as I tried to unpick her explanation. "You're saying that your son Owain created vampires?"

"No. Owain and his brothers were cursed. That led to the creation of Dark Ones. Did you not listen to me? I'd have thought that someone in your position would be more respectful of clients. Can you find Owain, or not?"

I thought of my almost nonexistent bank balance. I thought of Savian spending so much time over the last few days imparting to me his wisdom, and I thought about how miserable I was living in a small room in a gloomy student house.

"Yes, I can find him," I said, hoping I wasn't mistaken. "If he's related to vampires, he'll shed sanguine. I should be able to find that marker."

"What sanguine?" she asked. "What marker?"

"Every immortal has a marker trait that is unique to them. Demons leave demon smoke soot everywhere they go. My cousin Savian's wife is a dragon, so she leaves dragon scales. Dark Ones leave sanguine as a marker. It's kind of an arcane-based blood residue that thief takers can see. If you give me your address, I'll head right over and see if I can't catch his trail."

We spent a few more minutes discussing fees, timelines, and details concerning Owain's appearance. By the time I hung up, excitement had pushed ahead of the doubt that filled my mind, and I packed up my thief taker's kit (on loan from Savian until I had my own) and set off to a prestigious neighborhood half an hour's train ride away.

"I will show you the room where Owain was … er … staying," Jerry announced when I arrived, spinning around in the doorway in a manner that left me dodging her long blonde hair.

"That would be helpful," I said, studying the ground, searching for markers left by the missing Owain. Although there was a bit of sanguine trapped along the edges of the stairs that led to the front door, it was old, probably having been deposited about a week before. "Your son disappeared today, is that correct?"

"Yes. The last time I saw him was when I brought him breakfast. He still refused to see reason, so I left to visit a mage I hoped would help."

I followed her down a flight of stairs until we were in what I assumed used to be the domain of Georgian and Victorian servants, a space with a low stone ceiling and old gaslight fixtures side by side with more modern illumination. To the left a bank of grimy windows opened onto the service area just below street level, while on the right were three doors.

But it was the floor that held my interest. Once again, I saw nothing there but old sanguine.

"This was his room," Jerry said, opening a door and gesturing for me to go in.

I had been expecting something resembling a cell, given my suspicions Jerry was up to shenanigans, so to speak, but the room I stepped into was quite comfortable. Cozy, even, with an antique fireplace, a big leather recliner, a TV on the wall, and a large bed. A door led off to a lovely bathroom, while a floor-to-ceiling window looked out on an abandoned garden.

The floor was carpeted in sanguine, as was the bottom of the window frame.

"He left by the window," I said, examining it closer. It—matching the age of the house—was of an old Georgian style and, while appearing shut, wasn't locked. I gave it a little push, and the window swung on a central pivot, allowing a blast of cold air into the room. I ignored the icy weather and peered out through the window to the frozen ground below. We'd had a light dusting of snow a week or so before, but it had melted away during the daylight hours, leaving the ground frosty and hard.

While there weren't any footprints visible, the sanguine was there, leading away from the house.

"Dammit! I had three different types of wards on that window. Can you find him?" Jerry asked, shivering and rubbing her arms against the freezing air that swirled around us.

"I think so. At the very least, I'll give it my best shot," I answered, taking one last look at the trail before I closed the window. "It looks like there's a gate at the back of your garden, so he most likely left via it. The markers head that way, so I'll pop out back and make sure that's what happened, then hit the road and see what signs of him are there."

She murmured her agreement with that plan, and I quickly found myself out in a frosty, overgrown garden, grateful I hadn't yet needed to pawn my big woolen coat. I shoved my frozen fingers deep into the pockets and followed the trail across the lumpy lawn, my gaze on the little glimmers of red sanguine as they glittered in the weak winter sun, and wondered about the handsome man with gray eyes and hip-hop hair (I still had no idea what that was).

What had he taken from Jerry? Where was he going? And most worrying of all, why did I have the feeling he'd escaped from a bad situation?

"Keep your head down, and do your job," I told myself, parroting Savian's advice as I emerged from the garden to a street. Relief filled me at the sight of sanguine drifting across the road as cars passed, stirring it up. "Don't get involved in the clients' lives more than you have to. And certainly do not dwell on thoughts of just how handsome this man evidently is. You don't need a man complicating your life."

I hurried down the street, following the trail of markers, wondering what was the hip-hop hairstyle that Jerry had mentioned, and whether her son was as attractive as she claimed.

THREE
TATIANA

"Welcome to 'Axegate Walk: The Next Generation.' The shops are all located to the left, on the boardwalk, while on the right you'll find Dante Castle. A guided tour is included for those of you possessing a comprehensive day pass, including a visit to the grounds, and a cream tea in the new tearoom to the rear of the castle. This brochure includes a map of the Seventh Hour and has all the points of interest marked clearly, as well as their admittance times. Please note that rooms at the inns are all booked, so if you don't have a reservation, I'm afraid you can't spend the night here. Enjoy your visit, and mind the oxcarts."

I paused as I hustled by Jareth, the town crier. Though just three feet tall, she was a force to behold. In fact, her people-wrangling skills were so great, we'd immediately put her in charge of tourism, a job she recently told me she loved much more than announcing new arrivals to the Hour.

"Everything OK?" I asked, glancing around nervously. I felt like I had a target on me.

"Absolutely," she reassured me, handing out the glossy pamphlet I'd spent months making, highlighting all that the Hour had to offer. "The first bus of tourists finished unloading, and the second is due to roll in soon. What's wrong with you? You're as twitchy as a slug in a samba contest."

"It's the marching band," I told her, checking behind me again.

"What about them?" Jareth asked, tucking away her pamphlets in a courier bag when the last of the arrivals wandered off to see the shops and sights. The former town square—now a replica of Axegate Walk, the boardwalk from my hometown of Ravenfall—was bustling with not just tourists but also residents who were wheeling carts full of merchandise, snacks, medieval clothing, and various other offerings sure to tempt tourist hearts. "I haven't seen them since this morning at our run-through."

"Count yourself lucky. They've been following me around all day, insisting it'll be more entertaining for visitors if I have a personal soundtrack," I answered with another look over my shoulder. "They followed me around playing 'Tequila' aggressively at me all morning. I finally got rid of them by pretending to have explosive diarrhea."

She pursed her lips and eyed me.

"I'm fine," I told her. "No digestive issues at all."

"That's good, because the last thing we need is explosive anything happening in front of the tourists. Ah. That's the second bus. They're about five minutes out," she said after her phone pinged at her. "Do you want to greet them, or should I continue?"

"You are the best greeter in the Hour, and far more knowledgeable than me. Besides, I have to check the druid dancers are sober. Remind me to warn the inns they are no longer allowed to sell them barrels of anything alcoholic, especially mead. They get way too smashed on mead," I told her, unable to keep from turning to scan the people strolling along the boardwalk.

"I thought their interpretive dance of how you and Finch met and fell in love was touching," she said as I started off to a garden behind the biggest inn, where the druid tribal-dance team was residing in three yurts. "Although their version of the consummation of your relationship was a bit raunchy."

I sighed, remembering the banquet Finch and I had thrown for everyone the night before to celebrate the opening of the Hour to tourists. The druids had insisted on performing a dance that was wildly inappropriate at best. "They really have a lot to answer for. Right, I'm off to deal with them and the missing popcorn machine. Yell if you need anything."

I confirmed with the shop owners that everything was a go with them, and was heading for the inn when Finch began muttering in my head.

What's wrong? Why are you speaking in Czech, which you know I don't understand? Has something gone awry with the tea shop? They were fine half an hour ago, when I checked to make sure they were ready for the onslaught of tourists.

Come home, Tat.

Huh? I paused as I was about to verify that the three carriage drivers were ready to ferry tourists around to the various scenic points in the Hour that we'd included on the Romantic Underworld Horse-Drawn Carriage Experience. *Why? Are you moving up your Lord of the Hour speech? I really do think that would be better after the Dinner with a Vampire event. It'll have more impact then, don't you think?*

It has nothing to do with that blasted dinner you insist will be popular—

Might I remind you that those dinner tickets sold out in under four minutes? Four minutes, Finch. Everyone loves a sexy vamp, and you're the sexiest of all.

To my surprise, I didn't catch a sense of pleasure at my compliment, or even appreciation for the fact that we were madly in love despite being banished to the Hour. Instead, irritation, frustration, and even anger rolled around inside him. *We have visitors. Please come home so I don't do something I'll regret later.*

Has one of the tourists bothered you? I asked as I switched directions and quickly trotted through the town, my heart sinking when, from the shadows of the hot goat yoga salon, a brassy note greeted my appearance. The eight members of the marching band emerged, and immediately kicked into the only song they seemed to know.

I bolted, dodging tourists and residents as I headed to the small castle that we'd had built when we took over the Hour, a little more than a year before. *Dammit, the band found me! I'm coming in hot, Finch. Have the drawbridge ready to be yanked up the second I get across it.*

He sighed in my head. *Just tell them you don't want them following you.*

It's not that easy. They insist tourists love this sort of thing. One of them saw something similar on TikTok, and now they are convinced they are enhancing the tourist adventure. Why are you so annoyed? Did a tourist breach your inner sanctum and ask you to make them your eternal king or queen of the night? Because I'm happy to tell them you're quite taken, and you're not eternal nighting anyone but me.

He didn't answer, but I could feel him thinking several dark things.

The sound of "Tequila" followed me as I raced to get sufficiently ahead of the marching band so I could lose them, but other than them hitting some choppy notes as they picked up speed when I ran full out for a side door, they stuck to me.

By the time I hurried into Finch's library, located on the ground floor of the castle with a view over the town, I had imagined all sorts of outrageous scenarios, but I wasn't prepared at all for what I saw when I came to an abrupt halt in the middle of the library, the band triumphantly finishing as they crowded in after me.

Finch, gorgeous as ever, but particularly handsome in the tuxedo I'd managed to talk him into for the fancy (and expensive) dinner for eager tourists, stood next to two men, one tall with dark, curly hair, the other slighter, bearing an apologetic expression.

"—and I really don't like repeating myself, so if you could take yourself and your wife off, I'll get back to the business of leading the Hour," the first man was saying, shooting me an annoyed glance when I tucked my hand into the crook of Finch's arm. "It would appear you have musicians accompanying you. I do not have musicians. Leo!"

"Yes, sir." Leonid of Corinth, assistant to the Greek god Troy Ilios, wore an almost permanent expression of martyrdom. I gathered being Troy's flunky wasn't all it was cut out to be. "I'll look into a marching band for you, as well."

"These ones appear winded," Troy said as he gave the band a once-over. "Make sure that my musicians have some stamina and don't stand around panting like they ran a marathon. Now that your wife is here, we can proceed. I assume you have things here in this castle that I don't recall being consulted over before it was built. Leo will send your belongings on to you. Now, where is the media room? I have accepted a sponsorship that requires me to post videos every other day, and I want to get a few filmed before the light shifts."

"Troy Ilios," I said, making an abbreviated bow to the Greek god who had been the former head of the Hour. "And Leo, how nice to see you again. Are you here to see what we've done with the Hour? This is our grand opening to tourist trade, so things are a bit hectic—"

"They're here to kick us out, Tatiana," Finch said, his voice gravelly.

For what seemed like the millionth time in the last year, I mourned the loss of my Ravenfall boon, the trait given to me for being born in the small, highly eccentric town on the coast of Oregon.

I really did miss hearing the colors in people's voices. Finch's voice was almost always a rich forest green flecked with gold, both comforting and sexy as hell.

"Why?" I asked, confused, glaring when one of the trumpets tooted a fast fanfare, turning my attention to Troy. "Is it because we made our own version of Axegate Walk? Finch went over the rules of the Hour with a fine-tooth comb, and we didn't see anything that said we couldn't change the Hour's aesthetics—"

"No, no, I don't mind that," Troy answered, preening in front of a small mirror. "Some of the vistas will be excellent for filming direct conversations with my fans. I am simply reclaiming my position."

The trombones made a *wah-wah* noise.

"Begone!" Troy told them before I could demand they leave me alone, and to my utter stupefaction, they listened to him, the band members shooting me cheeky looks before they all filed out.

"How did you do that?" I couldn't help but ask.

"I am lord of the Hour," Troy said, giving me a one-shouldered shrug. "All here heed me."

"My question is why you want to be here. You told us you didn't want to lead the Hour any longer," Finch protested, his ire well and truly engaged now. "You claimed we had to pay for releasing the thane, and that we were responsible for keeping the other three contained, as well as tending to the rest of the occupants. We have done so to the best of our abilities."

Troy gave an abbreviated roll of his eyes. "You didn't think I meant for you to take the job permanently, did you? Leo! Did you not tell this Dark One that he was to mind the Hour for me while I was exploring what it was to be a social media star, and not take over the thing forever?"

"No, sir, I didn't tell him that. You seemed very adamant that you were done with the Hour, and wanted nothing more to do with it," Leo answered, shooting us an apologetic glance.

"As if I could do that even if I wanted, which I do not," Troy answered with a little snort. "I'm bound to the Hour by its articles of creation."

"You had me give Finch and Tatiana your seal," Leo pointed out.

"I know not of what you speak," Troy said, waving away the point in order to set up his phone on the mantel above the gorgeous antique fireplace that Finch had sourced from another Hour. He posed in front of it. "I am the lawful lord of the Hour. I have always been so, since the day it was created. Do you remember that day, Dark One? Of course you do not. You weren't here when that dragon and the Sovereign asked me to lead the Hour, not to mention the fact that you're not even a demigod, let alone a god like me. Everyone knows gods rule the twelve Hours. Leo, make sure that my band is here by the evening. I see there is a celebratory banquet scheduled, and the denizens of the Hour, as well as the tourists, will enjoy watching me listen to music."

Of all the pigheaded, conceited, narcissistic jerks, I muttered, wanting badly to do something extreme, like throw paint on Troy, ruining his expensive suit.

Do not, under any circumstances, aggravate him, Finch warned. *He may be treating us without thought, but as he pointed out, he is an actual god, and he has a prior claim on the Hour.*

"Yeah, but we did all the work," I complained out loud, wanting Troy and Leo to know how unfair it was for the former to come marching in and tell Finch we were no longer in charge.

Life, as my mother frequently said, is anything but fair, he murmured, allowing me to feel his own frustration with the situation.

I made a sharp gesture toward Troy. "We got all the paperwork together to bring in tourists, and we held countless town halls explaining to the residents about our idea, and everyone was super excited about Axegate Walk Underworld, and now we're supposed to walk away on opening day? It's not right!"

Troy held up a metal disk about three inches across. "I bear the seal. The Hour is mine by right and practice. Your time here is finished. You may return to the mortal world to do whatever it is you do there."

"That's ours! You took it from Finch's desk!"

I had a whole lot more to say when Troy tucked away the Hour's official seal, but Finch stopped me by taking my hand and giving my fingers a little warning squeeze.

"Even if we wished to leave—and as my Beloved said, we have worked for over a year to get the Hour to the state you find it—as residents of the Hour, we are technically dead, and can't return to the mortal world."

"Also, I'd like a guitar. I used to play it some sixty years ago—do you remember? I wore a turtleneck while I played romantic songs," Troy told Leo. "I will play the guitar for the tourists, and wear my turtleneck. My Instagram followers will love it, as well. What? That is a minor point, Dark One."

"Being dead might be a minor thing to you, but I assure you that Tatiana and I find it of great importance," Finch said, biting off the end of each word, which told me just how annoyed he was.

Annoyed doesn't begin to cover it.

Preaching to the choir, I told him.

"Fine," Troy said with an obvious roll of his eyes. "If you're going to be obstinate about it."

I opened my mouth to tell him that there was no way we were going to miss seeing the results of a year of our hard work when he waved a hand, a brilliant golden light poured over us, one that inexplicably filled me with joy, and then suddenly I was on my knees on a rough surface.

I looked up, for a moment too stunned to believe what I was seeing.

Finch?

Right here. He swore in Czech. *I don't believe it.*

"We're back?" I said, taking his offered hand, slowly getting to my feet as I looked around.

It was nighttime, but we were standing on a pavement, a salty breeze whipping around us. I took a deep breath, closing my eyes as I gave myself up to the moment.

We were home.

"Ravenfall," I said on a sigh, opening my eyes so I could fling myself on Finch, kissing him five times before releasing him to spin around, my hands jubilantly in the air. "We're back where we belong!"

"And we're alive," Finch said, incredulity giving his voice a distinct teal-blue tinge.

"Holy shit!" I yelled, turning back to him, goose bumps rippling down my arms. "You're teal!"

He looked down at himself. "I am?"

"Your voice! There's a teal overtone to your forest-green voice. Finch! My boon is back! We're alive, and I have my boon, and we're in Ravenfall. What the hell happened?"

I did a dance of happiness, wanting immediately to run down the streets to reacquaint myself with the town, and also to spirit him away to the nearest bed so I could have my way with him.

"The answer is Troy, obviously," Finch said, glancing around. There were a few people out on the street, but no one paid us any mind until a voice spoke behind us.

"Welcome home," a woman said, moving out of the shadows to pass by us. She was dressed in a sequined, body-hugging outfit that always reminded me of the singer P!nk. The fact that she also resembled the singer heightened the effect, but I knew there was much more to her than a love of music.

"Your Grace," Finch said, making one of the bows that he pulled off with such style. "It is a pleasure to see you again."

It was Anya, one of the three beings who made up the Municipal Entity, the people in charge of Ravenfall.

Finch had speculated that at least one of them had a lot of power, and I firmly believed it was Anya.

"Always so polite," she said with a smile at Finch before her gaze moved to me. "You will no doubt be taking over the shop you left with your cousin. We will see to the change in ownership. We have not been happy to have the shop closed so much, and welcome your return."

"The shop's closed? Clemmie didn't say anything about leaving it." I consulted my phone, but found the last text from my twenty-year-old cousin was a few weeks old.

"I believe she mentioned something about attending a college in California to learn how to make"—she paused for a moment, clearly pulling something out of her memory—"artistic horror rom-coms. I did not know such a thing was a genre, but evidently your cousin feels it's her calling. Good evening."

She glided off in the direction of the town hall. We both stared after her for a few seconds before turning to each other.

"We're back," I told Finch, feeling stupidly stuck on that point.

"We are. Alive. That should make things easier for us to find our missing thane."

"You think we still have to find him?" I asked, some of my pleasure fading at the memory of the man we'd inadvertently released. "Maybe he died or something. If your uncle hasn't heard hide nor hair of the big, bad Owain, then perhaps he's not a real threat, and we can enjoy being alive again, and back in Ravenfall."

"I believe the phrase is *seen* hide nor hair. ..."

The look I gave Finch was so pointed, the corners of his lips curled.

"Regardless of your choice in creative phrasing, the thane is an immense threat to not just Dark Ones but the mortal world, as well. We have no choice but to work with my uncle to find Owain before he commits atrocities upon everyone. And that drives home the point that I must call my uncle immediately to find out where he is in the search, and what we can do to help." Finch took my hand as we started down the sidewalk toward the shop that he used to rent and later bought for Clemmie's livelihood.

A little frisson of worry formed in my belly. Finch might be a proficient fighter, but I had qualms about him tackling the thane on his own. I hoped the other vampires had a plan in place to catch the madman.

I wasn't about to risk the man who held my heart. Not again.

FOUR
BERRY

"Where did you lose your vampire?"

"Train station. St. Pancras." I glanced around a statue of two lovers embracing, my spirits forlorn when I saw no sign of vampire markers on the ground, a few scattered dragon scales, some arcany that indicated a fairly large group of mages had passed through, and even a few markers from an earth elemental. "The trail was clear until I got to the station. I've searched all the floors, but there's nothing. Savian—I really don't want to fail my very first job, but I don't know what to do."

"Hmm. That's the international hub." His voice was thoughtful, and he was quiet for so long that I glanced at my phone to make sure it hadn't dropped the call. "I don't like that."

"I'm screwed, aren't I?" I sighed. "He's probably in Europe by now, and I'll never find him, and that scary Dr. Kostich will kick my ass out, and I'll have to go back to doing mortal work, because no one wants a bad knocker with a reputation for failure."

"While I admire the depths of the pity pool into which you have sunk, I don't think it's as dire a situation as that," Savian answered, amusement rich in his voice. "It's daytime, and most vampires don't like to travel when they have to be out in the sun."

"I'm not sure this guy is actually a vampire," I said slowly, thinking over what Jerry had told me. "His mom called him a thane, and said he was one of her four sons who formed the race of vampires. Or rather, Dark Ones."

"If he made them, then he's bound to have the same traits as them," Savian argued. "Regardless, I'll make a call and have one of the sprites I use help find his trail."

"Sprites? The little girls from the Court of Divine Blood?" I asked, confused why I would want someone from what most mortals thought of as heaven. "I don't see how they can help."

"I was planning on discussing sprites as aides in locating markers in our next thief taker lesson, but it sounds like I'd better do it now. Although, yes, they do frequently take the appearance of young girls, my go-to team of trackers usually look like twenty-somethings. Why, I can hear you thinking to yourself, do sprites help? The answer is simple: they can see markers that are too faint for you and me. Where, exactly, are you in St. Pancras?"

"First floor, near the statue of the lovers," I answered, a faint glow of hope blossoming to life within me.

"Stay there. I'll send Tarantella to you. She's in England, and can get to you quickly via the Beyond."

I hung up, wondering about beings who could travel in the alternate version of reality known as the Beyond, but decided I wouldn't question any help, no matter whom it came from.

Almost half an hour later, a young woman sat down on the bench beside me. She had turquoise-and-pink hair done in braids that hung to her waist, wore bright-yellow overalls, and bore a pair of oversized sunglasses that reminded me of pictures of Jackie Onassis.

"Hi. I'm Tara. Savian said you need some help finding a vamp?"

"Yes, please," I said, tucking away my phone. I'd been searching for information about exactly what a vampire thane was, but there was nothing online. "I'm at a loss as to where he could have gone."

"Let's see where you looked already," she said, getting back to her feet. I took her down to the ground floor, retracing my earlier movements as I searched that floor, the mezzanine, and the upper level. "The only markers I saw were at the door and inside the entrance. But after that, zzzt. The trail goes cold."

"There's certainly no sign of your thane up here," Tara said as she slowly paced, her gaze scanning the floor ahead of us. "So I think you can stop worrying that he took a train out of the country. Let's go back to the entrance. I want to take another look at the pattern of sanguine there."

I didn't see how that would help, but I wasn't a super tracker, so I followed her downstairs, and watched as she searched the entrance where I'd seen the sanguine. There was less of it visible now, no doubt due to the dispersal generated by so many people passing through the area, but to my surprise, after about fifteen minutes, Tara suddenly stood up from where she'd been doubled over, examining the floor. "Got him. This way!"

I trotted after her when she ran down a side passage toward the bathrooms and administrative offices.

"See here? He paused at the toilets, then stood for a short time on the corner before heading this way. I wonder why ... ah." The administrative hallway split, one side leading to a dead end filled with trash bins, while the other clearly held offices. "Here's where he ended up for a bit."

I wrinkled my nose at the massive trash container. "Ew."

"I'm willing to bet it wasn't for the ambience. The sanguine is pooled like he stood here for five or ten minutes, but someone else was here with him. There's two voids in the marker pattern that can only be the feet of another person."

"Was he hiding with someone?" I asked, more confused than ever. I studied the ground but only saw the very faintest of shimmer indicating the sanguine Owain the thane had shed.

"He's a Dark One, right?" She gave a little shrug before starting back the way we'd come. "He was probably feeding from some mortal. OK, now that I have his marker down, I can see his exit path. The game is afoot!"

It took about twenty minutes, but at last I was able to see the trail that Tara had followed out of the train station, and down to Russell Square. "You're brilliant, and are a godsend," I thanked her when I had been able to follow the trail on my own for a block. "Er … how much do I owe you?"

"Not a thing other than a good review on my Court of Divine Blood profile page," she said with a bright smile. "Your cousin has me on retainer, and it was the least I could do for him, since he's laid up for a week or so."

"He is a good guy," I agreed, glancing around the area. "I wonder what the thane is doing in this area. It doesn't scream vampire hunting grounds to me."

Tara gave a half shrug. "The British Museum is just over there. Maybe he went in it. There's also an entrance to Abaddon a couple of blocks from here, but I can't imagine why he'd want to go there. Welp, if you don't need me for anything else, I'll pop back to the Court. My aunt is Sovereign, and I promised her I'd help with a problem she has concerning some mages. See ya!"

I thanked her again, and stood for a moment wondering what Owain the thane was doing, and whether he was going to give me any trouble once I found him, but decided it was a waste of energy worrying about the unknown.

The markers were fairly visible as I followed their trail to the south, before I came to a dead end at a small red-and-white brick building. There was no obvious sign of its purpose, but the sanguine ended at the door. I took a few steps back to eye the building, noting that the two upper floors looked uninhabited, its windows crusted with dirt and bits of dead ivy.

But what gave away the truth about the building was the sense of a thick, stifling presence that I recognized as dark power. This had to be the entrance to Abaddon that Tara had mentioned. I hesitated, glancing up and down the quiet street, lined with scattered small shops located on the ground floors, but with few people to be seen.

"Right. I'm an employee of the Committee, and as such, a treaty with Abaddon guarantees my safe passage to and from its scary self. Let's do this."

My feet refused to move for a good two minutes, but at last I psyched myself up and entered the house, immediately finding myself in a long, dark hallway. I braced for the presence of demons who would no doubt try to give me grief, but as I clutched my Committee identity card in one hand and a bottle of pepper spray in the other, I realized something shocking.

The hall was absolutely silent. Although I'd never been to Abaddon before, I had friends and relatives who had, and they all said the place was teeming with beings of dark powers, most notably the demons belonging to the ranks of the seven princes who ran the place.

"Hello?" My voice came out thin and reedy. I cleared my throat, flipped off the top of the pepper spray, and said a little louder, "Is anyone there? I'm looking for a vampire. A thane. If anyone has seen him, I'd appreciate knowing."

"Why?"

The voice that echoed down the hallway was hollow and masculine, with sharp edges that had me backing up a couple of steps. I'd heard tales of some super sort of demon who was almost as powerful as a demon lord himself, and this voice sounded like it fit the bill.

"Why am I looking for the vamp, or why would I appreciate knowing his whereabouts? If it's the latter, I've been hired to find him."

A shadow appeared midway down the hall, no doubt from a junction that I couldn't see. It was male-shaped, and looked to be a good four inches taller than me, which, since I was almost six feet tall, was no mean feat.

"Who hired you?"

The man had an English accent, and the sort of deep voice that rumbled down the hallway. It made me feel things, that voice, but I quickly quelled that response, since there was no way I wanted to admire anyone who lived in Abaddon.

"Yeah, that's not something I'm going to tell you," I said, my fingers tightening around my pepper spray as the shadow started down the hallway toward me.

"Client confidentiality and all that. Have you seen the thane?"

"Who are you?" the man asked, coming close enough that I could see he was dressed all in black: black jeans, a black shirt, and a black pea jacket. But it was his eyes that caught my attention and held it—his irises were pale gray, so pale they were almost white, with a pronounced thick black ring around the outer edge. "And why do you seek me? Deus, it was my mother, wasn't it?"

"Owain?" I said, noting that as Jerry had described, he had salt-and-pepper hair, the front of it swooping back in a wave that made my stomach tighten.

I still didn't understand why she called his hair hip-hop, but that aside, Jerry was right: he was handsome.

I couldn't tell if it was his jaw—angled in a way that made me feel a bit wobbly about the knees—or maybe the way his eyes seemed to pierce through me straight down to my soul, or if it was his wide, mobile mouth.

I tried hard not to stare at the lovely curve of his bottom lip, reminding myself that I had a job to do, and that did not include ogling my target.

"Who are you?" he repeated, his voice taking on harder edges. He stopped directly in front of me, his eyes going first to the pepper spray, then to the card held in my left hand.

Without waiting for my brain to kick in and supply an answer, he plucked the card from my fingers.

"Berengaria Anastasia North," he read, glancing from it to my face. "Provisional thief taker. Ah. It *was* my mother who sent you to find me. Is she outside, waiting to capture me? I'm surprised she didn't come in with you, although I suppose her ties to the Court of Divine Blood prohibit that. Well, I won't have it. I refuse to—one moment."

"Huh?" I asked, damning myself for being so stunned by his appearance that inanities were the only thing I was able to speak. I cleared my throat and said, "That is, yes, Jerry sent me, although I think she wants to talk to you, not enact a capture."

In the distance, I could faintly hear a feminine voice, although I couldn't tell what it was saying.

"No, you don't have to go to the palace itself. I already looked. It's empty. Come back, I'm about to escape the clutches of a thief taker that Jericho sent after us." Owain turned back to face me. "I have no further desire to speak with my mother. If you would step aside, I'll be on my way. Abaddon is empty."

"Huh?" I asked again, then shook my head madly. "Jeezumcrow, the place has me sounding like an idiot. What do you mean it's empty? It can't be empty. It's full of demons. It's always full of demons."

A bird whipped around the corner of the hall, careened into the far wall, righted itself, and continued flying straight at us in a lopsided manner.

"I don't even know why you insisted on coming here looking for Desislav the Destroyer. We could be at home, where I can sit by the fire and thaw out from this horrible weather. Goddess above, was there ever such a climate?" the bird said as she alighted on Owain's shoulder, bobbing her head a few times as she caught sight of me. "What's a knocker doing here?"

"Looking for Owain," I answered, wondering why a vampire would have a raven as a pet.

He took a step back. "You heard Orla?"

"The bird? Yeah. I'm a knocker, like she said. We can understand birds, not that they are usually chatty about anything but telling other birds how fabulous they are. I can also understand some foxes, although not the ones to the north. Their accent is beyond me. Hello, Orla. My name is Berry, and I don't want anyone captured, let alone your … er … friend."

"Friend?" Orla said with a squawk, doing a little dance on Owain's shoulder. "Gaoler is more like it."

"You are absolutely free to go wherever you want," Owain said, taking a step toward me. "Don't let me stop you from blighting someone else's life."

Her eyes glittered with a wicked light. "I'm not leaving until you break my curse and give me the talisman you made!"

"Allow me to pass, madam," Owain said, ignoring Orla.

"I wish I could, but your mother is concerned about you." I studied his face, which was certainly no hardship. The closer he got, the more attractive he was.

I even liked the fan of crow's-feet on the sides of his striking eyes. Sexy, sexy stubble and a cleft chin added to what I feared might be the undoing of my good intentions.

"I am perfectly fine now that I'm out of her clutches," he answered.

Orla the raven snorted.

"What did you say?" Owain asked her.

"I snorted. The idea of you being anything but deranged is snort-worthy," she said in a speed that, were she human, I would say was snapping.

"I'm so confused," I said, managing to wrestle my eyes off Owain and onto the very odd raven. "Why are you standing on his shoulder if you don't like him?"

"He cursed me!" she said in a near shriek, bobbing up and down again. "He cursed me after he tried to molest me!"

I raised my eyebrows at Owain.

He looked like he was about to roll his eyes, but managed to stop himself in time. "I did no such thing. Well, yes, it is true I cursed her, but only because she tried to kill me repeatedly for a month after I rejected her advances. I feel a little cursing is justified after seventeen attempts at murdering me."

"A raven tried to have sex with you?" I asked, well beyond confused and straight into the land of befuddlement.

"I wasn't a raven then!" Orla said in a near snarl. "I was a beauteous maiden, long of hair, and straight of limbs, and with plentiful baps that were the envy of all with working eyes! And it wasn't seventeen—it was only sixteen times. That incident with the poison was an accident. I was trying to take care of that annoying milkmaid who looked at you with lust in her eyes, and you drank the mead meant for her, instead."

Owain's expression turned to pure martyrdom.

"OK," I said slowly, eyeing the bird. "So, you and your baps and hair and all the rest of you wanted Owain, but he didn't want you?"

"I did not. Please move. If Desi is not in Abaddon, he must be out in the mortal world. I will have to find …" He paused, and gave me an impersonal once-over.

Annoyed with myself for caring what he thought of me, I squared my shoulders and tried to appear like I had better posture than my normal slouch.

"You said you were a thief taker.," he continued. "That means you can find people."

I backed up until I ran up against the door to the outside. "I am, and it does, although I'm only a provisional thief taker, and if you're thinking I can find this Desi dude for you, I'd like to point out I already have a job: to find you."

"You have done so," he pointed out, reaching around me and opening the door, forcing me to take a couple of steps forward until I was almost pressed against him. "Your job is completed. You can now take mine. I wish for you to locate Desislav. I will aid you in the search, since he is powerful and dangerous."

"Freedom!" Orla screeched, and flew past me to a tree in a cement planter.

I looked up at Owain, once again admiring his face, and eyes, and that delicious lower lip, and for a few seconds, all I could think of was how good he smelled, and how much I wanted to run my hands through his hair. "I ... your mom seems concerned about you. ..."

"She isn't, you know," he said, leaning in until his scent wrapped around me. His pupils flared, darkening his eyes even as I suddenly seemed to forget how to breathe. "She wants something from me, a gift she gave me almost two thousand years ago. And if she gets it, Desislav the Destroyer will have the means to throw me back into the Seventh Hour with my brothers. I will not go back to captivity, either one of my mother's making or that of a self-obsessed Greek god who runs the Hour."

"The Seventh Hour? The underworld one?" I asked, a sense of righteous indignation mingling with confusion and pure lust.

Lust? I thought back. Had it really been three years since I'd had a romantic partner? Where had the time gone?

"The very same. If you were planning on visiting, I would urge you to think otherwise. Their prison is dismal at best. At least the gaol my mother confined me to had a television and computer to while away the hours of imprisonment."

While he spoke, he more or less forced me outside onto the pavement.

"Who's Desislav the Destroyer? And what sort of mother holds her son prisoner?"

"One who is obsessed with striking a blow against Cernunnos," he answered.

"The Irish Cernunnos? Lord of the hunt?" I asked, more confused than ever.

"Come," he said, blithely disregarding my question to gesture down the street. "I have obtained a secure room nearby. We will make plans for locating Desi and his blood moon."

"Yeah, I may look like an idiot—" I started to say.

"No, you look incompetent," Orla said, alighting again on Owain's shoulder as he hustled me forward. "And also, you're huge. When did people get so big?"

"—but I assure you that I wasn't born yesterday, and I am most certainly not going into a room alone with you," I finished with only one glare at the bird.

"Very well," he said, and veered off to the left, a hand on my arm making sure I came with him. "There is a restaurant a few blocks from here run by dragons. We will discuss your search for Desi there, where you will feel secure. Orla, you may not speak offensively to our thief taker. I believe your misbehavior qualifies as needing a time-out."

To my astonishment, he drew a symbol on the air that hung glittering pale blue for a few seconds before it dissolved into nothing, taking Orla with it even as she was screaming, "Nooooo!"

"What—"

"I sent her into the Beyond," he answered. "She'll be back when she can find her way out of it, which can take a day if I'm lucky. Regardless, we will be able to discuss the situation concerning Desi without her being obnoxious."

Despite being annoyed with his high-handed treatment, I was grateful not only for the fact he dealt with the bad-tempered bird, but also that he chose a place where I wouldn't be isolated and potentially vulnerable.

Vulnerable to the lure of his incredibly sexy self, I thought, but quickly dismissed the idea of touching his hair, and possibly chest, and most definitely running a finger down the angled line of his jaw just before I kissed the breath right out of him.

"May I remind you again that I'm a thief taker, and I couldn't possibly tackle someone who is known as 'the Destroyer.' If he has something to do with Abaddon, then he's likely pretty powerful, and powerful people don't like it when you track them down."

Owain paused to give me an extremely pointed look.

"OK," I said, not in the least bit intimidated, although it was obvious he expected me to be. I wondered briefly at the fact that he didn't strike me as dangerous when he most likely was—I mean, you don't help create a brand-new race of beings unless you have some pretty significant powers. "I admit that came out borderline insulting. I assure you I'm not slighting you or what I assume is your badass reputation. It's … well, if we're being honest, you're not the sort of scary that I imagine this Desi guy is. I assume he's a demon lord? Or adjacent to one? Is he one of those wrath demons who are almost demon-lord level of bad?"

"I like how you think," Owain told me, taking me by complete surprise. "Your mind is refreshing."

"Refreshing in a good way, like you enjoy a good stream of consciousness, or refreshing as in you want to eat my brains? You don't look like a revenant, but admittedly, I haven't been around any of them, so I can't be sure. Wait, you *are* a vampire, yes? Because your mother didn't say you were, exactly, but the sprite who helped me find you said that if you formed vamps, you must have the same sort of traits. But it's sunny out, and you aren't skulking from shadow to shadow to avoid being burned to a crisp. Plus you haven't tried to drink my blood. Was it because you topped up at St. Pancras? You do drink blood, right?"

Owain had continued walking as soon as I responded, once again with a hand firmly holding on to my arm. He waited until my verbal wanderings dribbled to a stop before saying, "I will answer your questions, but only because you are nervous, and I wish to show you that I will never harm you."

"Never?" I asked before he could continue, slanting a glance up at his pretty eyes.

"Never," he repeated.

"What if I went Van Helsing on you, and tried to stake you?" I asked.

"Then I'd stop you. Do you want me to answer your questions or not?"

We were standing at a traffic light, with only a couple of people ahead of us. So as not to be overheard, I scooted a step closer to him, once again reveling in his spicy cologne, which wrapped around my head and made my libido roar to life. "Go ahead and answer the first lot of questions. I have more."

"I had a feeling you did," he said with a flicker of the martyred expression he'd worn earlier. That made me want to giggle, but since that might be insulting, I kept it to myself. "I will answer in the order you asked. I find the way you think refreshing because most mortals I've met since I was expulsed from the Hour do not make me want to laugh."

"I made you want to laugh?" I asked, dumbfounded.

He looked anything but amused.

"Yes," he said, his expression deadpan. "Next, I am not a revenant nor a Dark One. With my three brothers, we attempted to destroy Abaddon. Our punishment for such an act was a bloodlust curse. My brothers and I all had sons—I had two, Rhain had more than twenty, Rhys had three, and Cadell had one. As such, the terms of the curse laid our sins upon our sons, and it was those approximately thirty sons who were the first Dark Ones."

"Your brother had twenty sons?" Incredulity no doubt filled my expression. "And also, you have two kids? Are you … eh … married? Involved with someone?"

"I'm still answering the first set of questions," he said as we waited at yet another red light. "But yes, I have two sons. I'm unsure of the exact number of Rhain's spawn, but the last I heard, they numbered over twenty. He took great pleasure in bedding as many women— and some men—as he could. We did not have recognized marriages as you know it when I was with my sons' mother, but she was the equivalent to a wife until she died in childbirth. I mourned her loss for many centuries."

"I'm so sorry," I said as we hurried across the street. I wanted to say something comforting, but I didn't know what wouldn't sound trite. "It's never easy to lose a loved one, and I can imagine that losing her to childbirth was especially devastating."

"It was not a good time, no," he agreed, pointing when we came to another intersection. "That is the dragons' restaurant, on the right. As for your other questions, I do not share the traits of Dark Ones other than I must drink blood to survive, and the sun isn't overly kind to me if I remain out in it for a protracted length of time. As the left side of my face is starting to sting, I will need to take refuge inside for a while, so it's good we're almost to our destination."

I glanced at the side of his face nearest me. He did look a bit pink, like he was starting to sunburn. "Oh, crap. OK, let's hurry to the restaurant."

"Finally, your sprite was correct. I found a gullible mortal from whom I fed an hour ago, which is one reason why I have not pounced on you to swill back your blood."

I stared at him in open-mouthed horror for a few seconds as my own thoughts were spoken aloud. Then I realized how idiotic I looked. "Swill back … I was just … you can read minds?"

"Not normally, no," he answered, holding open the door to the restaurant.

I took a quick look in to make sure it wasn't some sort of setup where I'd be vulnerable to attack either by Owain or by someone else (everyone knew dragons were very clannish, and didn't help others without some pretty heavy payment).

Fortunately, it appeared to be a perfectly normal restaurant with booths on one side of its L-shaped interior, while the other was dotted with small round tables and chairs.

It was about half-full of diners, so I allowed Owain to escort me inside. "Well, you did poke around in my mind, and frankly, I don't like it."

He cocked an eyebrow at me, making my stomach do an odd excited flip-flop. "Would that be because you were mentally referring to me as 'an almighty bloodsucker' or because you like my lower lip?"

The blush hit me hard and fast. As someone with jet-black hair and dark tan skin inherited from my Egyptian mother, I don't show blushes very well, but I was afraid he could feel the heat radiating from my face. "I'd apologize about that, but I believe everyone is entitled to their own thoughts. However, if it makes you feel uncomfortable, I will try to refrain from thinking about your lip when you're nearby." My voice sounded stilted as hell, but I was dying of embarrassment inside.

"I agree," he said, glancing around the interior of the restaurant, obviously one of those people who scopes out exits when entering a new place. For some reason, I felt itchy, as if I could feel his emotion of heightened awareness of my surroundings.

"You do? About what?" I couldn't help but ask.

"You have the right to privacy with your thoughts. I will not mention your obsession with my lip and jaw again. Hello. Yes, two of us. Could we sit somewhere away from mortals?" The last was spoken to a woman who approached with a couple of menus.

She smiled at us both. "Our doors are warded to prohibit entrance to mortals who are not familiar with the Otherworld. This way, please."

I seethed to myself over the fact that he'd somehow overheard my thoughts about his jaw, as well as his lip, and I caught myself wondering if he knew about my desire to run my hands through his hair before I clamped down on that desire, too, watching him closely for signs he was actively reading my thoughts.

One side of his mouth twitched, but I doubted if it meant anything. "Be back in a minute. I need to use the restroom. Er …"

"Left at door," the waitress said, pointing to the other side of the restaurant.

I murmured my thanks, and feeling moderately guilty—but mindful of the oath I'd taken when I was accepted as a thief taker—I quickly texted to Jericho the fact that I'd found her son, he was not harmed in any way, and we were going to spend a little time at a dragon restaurant.

"It's my job," I told myself as I returned to the far end of the restaurant, pushing down the guilt that rose at the sight of Owain.

Dammit, I couldn't fall for someone I'd just met. He was the focus of my job, that's all. I had to remember what was important: my nascent career, and not a handsome, troubled man who seemed to have a connection to me that I couldn't quite pinpoint ... and I wasn't sure I wanted to.

Sometimes, ignorance really is bliss.

FIVE
BERRY

"I am happy to pay for your lunch," Owain said, nodding toward the menu when I sat down opposite him. "You look hungry."

"I don't look anything of the sort," I argued, despite the fact that I was near ravenous after having had only a yogurt for breakfast. My salary from the Committee wouldn't hit my bank account for another few weeks, and Jericho wouldn't pay me until I produced her son, which meant I was on an unavoidable diet.

He raised that damned eyebrow again, and I thought a great many rude things at the same time I consulted the menu. "Fine, I'm a bit peckish, but I do not *look* hungry, although … well, it is nice of you to offer to treat me. Thank you. Can you not eat food?"

"I can, but it doesn't provide me with any nutrients. I must take in blood to survive. Why are you embarrassed about enjoying my lip and jaw and hair? I feel no such embarrassment looking at you."

I sat up very straight, shooting him my best piercing glare, about to unleash my thoughts upon him when he stopped me dead in my tracks by placing his hand over mine, which was clutching the menu with fingers made white with anger.

"Do not lash me with your words. I simply meant that I am not embarrassed by the pleasure I take in looking at your face and … er … other parts. You are quite comely, and I admire your mouth, as well. Also, your hair. It is blacker than Orla's feathers, and is glossy, like a shiny piece of hematite."

Warmth blossomed in my belly at the compliment, but it was quickly ruined by guilt, touched with a bit of annoyance. It was a confusing mix of emotions that I didn't know how to process. "I … OK, that was nice, thank you, but you don't get to comment on my body. That's not cool."

"Not even if it is a compliment?" he asked, his eyes steady on mine, and I realized with a jolt that he was actually interested in my answer. He wasn't just bull-shitting me to get me to work for him.

Now I felt worse than ever that I'd told his mom I'd found him. I tried desperately to think of some way out of the difficult situation without ruining my burgeoning career, but short of admitting what I'd done, I didn't see any other option. "Strictly speaking, no. Although … well, I guess I compliment people sometimes, and I don't mean anything bad by it. I suppose I'll let your comment about my other parts pass. For now."

"Do you find compliments offensive?" he asked, pausing until the server took my order for a plate of spaghetti Bolognese. "Do you have body dysmorphia?"

"No," I said, trying to hide the fact that I was pulling down my shirt at the same time I squared my shoulders. "I am quite comfortable with my appearance."

"Good," he said, pulling out his phone. "May I have your number?"

"Sure." I handed him my phone so he could add his number to mine while I munched on the green salad that had been delivered. I tried hard not to stuff the whole thing in my mouth, and instead eat with at least a hint of civility. Not even remorse at finding myself in such an untenable situation could completely quell the ravages of hunger.

"Since I feel mildly awkward eating in front of you, why don't you tell me about this Desislav guy, and why you want me to find him?" I suggested, fighting to keep from diving face-first into the delicious spaghetti when it was placed before me.

"Very well." He leaned back in the chair, his gaze taking another trip around our end of the restaurant. "Desislav the Destroyer, along with two other men who later became princes of Abaddon, used a relic known as the blood moon to form Abaddon. Centuries later, my brothers and I were born, and after dealing with our mother's father—he was a druid—and his kin, we became aware that Abaddon was having a greater effect on mortals than was safe."

I managed to keep from moaning at the taste of the food, but it was a close thing. "Can you give me an idea of the time this happened? Was it, like, thousands of years ago, or within the memory of modern man?"

"Modern? No. As best I can pinpoint, it was about the year the mortals call two hundred CE."

"Gotcha." I eyed the garlic bread the waitress brought, and gave in to its carby lure, munching it as I asked, "So, you and your brothers wanted to protect the mortals? Or did you have another reason for closing down Abaddon?"

"It was wholly for the benefit of the mortal world." He thought for a moment, and I couldn't help but admire yet again how handsome he was. The corners of his mouth quirked. "And the immortal world, since the princes were testing the limits of their powers outside of Abaddon. Unfortunately, my brother Rhain believed we weren't strong enough to go against all three princes, not with Desi holding the blood moon. So he convinced us to draw upon our druid grandfather's clan, and also involve mortals in the planned destruction."

"Why mortals?" I asked, this time waiting before I swallowed to speak. "Aren't they powerless compared to demon lords?"

"By themselves, yes, but as thanes, our origins lie deep in the mortal races, and we gain our power from them. Rhain felt that with their backing, we would be able to do what we couldn't do alone."

"But it wasn't enough?" I asked, waiting for him to look down to his hands before stuffing a big wad of spaghetti into my mouth.

I might have to eat in front of the man, but it didn't mean I had to make a pig of myself.

"It may well have been, but we will never know. The mortals betrayed us, and the Court of Divine Blood—you know of the Court, yes?"

I nodded.

"The Court, which at that time was heavily involved in working to make the immortal and mortal races live together in harmony, decided that we were putting the mortals at risk, and threw their support in with Desi and the two other princes to defeat us."

"Heaven joined up with hell to destroy you guys?" I asked, my fork now frozen halfway to my mouth. "How on earth did that work? Also, that's horrible! Did you tell them that you guys were trying to help the mortals, not crush them?"

"I do not know what deal the Court made with Abaddon, but I have heard a rumor that the Sovereign at the time knew Desi personally, and that it was she who was responsible for the Court siding against us." He wiggled his shoulders a few times, as if he was stiff. "They weren't incorrect that the mortals who were to work with us would be at risk, but we had sworn to do all we could to protect them from the wrath of Abaddon."

"Were they, for lack of a better phrase, cannon fodder? The mortals, that is?" I asked, setting down my fork. "Is that why the Court thought you were putting them in danger?"

"No. I told you that thanes' power is sourced in mortal beings. It would be counterproductive to destroy that which gave us our abilities."

"How do they do that? I'm sorry if I'm diverting the discussion, but how do you get power from mortals?"

He shrugged. "How do you talk to birds? It is something that is bred into us. A few years ago, my brother Cadell was raging against our confinement, and likened mortals to batteries that gave us the ability to power our form of magic. I suppose that is as apt a description as any."

My sympathy for him grew, which in turn made regret at texting his mom all that much more painful. "So, everyone turned against you four, and Desi tossed you into the Seventh Hour?"

"More or less, yes. A few hundred years later, Desi himself was condemned to the Thirteenth Hour. We thought that was the end of it—he was gaoled, just as we were. But more importantly, his relic was no longer in his possession, so when I was expulsed from the Hour, I could focus on lifting the blood curse placed on us without fear of repercussion by Desi." His jaw worked a couple of times. "Then my mother informed me that not only had he been freed from his prison, but the blood moon was still in circulation, and was being sought by everyone. That is why I must have you find it, first."

Guilt rose up and swamped me until it made it hard for me to breathe.

"Wait, I thought you wanted me to find Desislav?" I asked, shaking my head when the waitress asked if I wanted anything else. I avoided looking at the half-empty plates that she removed from before me, regretting the loss of a good meal, but knowing it would all turn to the proverbial ashes in my mouth.

His lips tightened. "I do, although I want to know the location of the blood moon more. Without it, I am vulnerable to being sent back to my imprisonment in the Hour. I have spent almost two thousand years there. I don't wish to return. It would also allow me to break the curse on my brothers and me, although I doubt it would help existing Dark Ones. Still, it's another reason to ensure no one else gets the relic."

"Oh, goddess," I said, clutching my head for a moment in order to hide the shame at my actions. "What have I done? Owain, I'm sorry, but I … goddess, I've screwed everything up, but I was trying to do my job. My cousin Savian told me how important it is to not fail clients, and how the Commaittee takes a stand about thief takers who don't honor contracts, but this isn't right. You're a nice guy. I mean, I've only known you for what, half an hour? But I can tell you're nice. You take care of a bitchy bird who tried to kill you, and you brought me here where I'm safe, and what did I do to repay that kindness?"

He stilled at my words, a frozen look on his face. "Why are you consumed with guilt? What have you done?"

"I texted your mom we were having lunch," I admitted, so miserable I wanted to cry. "I didn't realize—I didn't know you had suffered so much. She said it was important I find you as quickly as possible, so I assumed that meant you were at risk. But you're not, are you?"

He was on his feet even before I finished my sorrowful admission. "I am if she gets her way. When did you tell her? When you went to the toilet?"

I nodded.

He closed his eyes for a few seconds before he marched toward the front of the restaurant.

I followed, desperate to do something to make up for my actions. He paused long enough to pay for my meal before asking the server, "Is there a back way out?"

The woman, who I realized with a start was a blue dragon, tipped her head to the side as she studied first Owain, then me. "Yes," she said finally, nodding toward the back area containing the bathrooms. "Through the garden."

Owain turned toward me, and I braced myself for the tongue-lashing I deserved, but before he had taken a step toward me, what I can only describe as a whirlwind made up of ravens swirled outside the door, the noise of their wings as they flew in a tight vertical cone formation filling the air.

"The Morrigna!" Owain grabbed my arm, and without a hesitation, we were moving through the restaurant, deftly avoiding both those dining and the handful of servers.

"What is—" I started to ask.

"Another name for an entity consisting of my mother and two of her sisters," he said in a near snarl, hurrying through the restaurant before jerking open a door that led to a small garden space, now filled with round wooden tables and chairs. At the back, a wrought iron gate led out to an alley.

"Oh, shit. She's here already? I'm sorry, Owain, I truly am. I feel sick about this. I'll talk to her, OK? I'll tell her that you're fine, and not in any danger—"

"She doesn't give a damn about that," he said, pushing me through the gate to the alley. "All she wants from me is her boon. This way."

He didn't bother asking; he took my hand and hauled me away from the garden.

"What boon? You have a boon?" I stumbled as I glanced back, and saw with horror the swarm of ravens round the corner of the building, heading straight for us. "Ack! The birds are following us! Maybe I should talk to them?"

"Under no circumstances are you to do that," he said, and again took me by surprise as he spun around, releasing my hand to position himself in front of me.

The raven tornado sped forward, caws scraping across the sky as it headed for us, the noise resolving itself into the same words, repeated in a chant. "The Morrigna, the Morrigna, the Morrigna comes."

"What are you doing?" I asked, trying to move around Owain, but he more or less shoved me behind him.

"Protecting you from them. Stay back. Do not talk to them. Do not listen to them. And above all, do not agree to anything they ask of you."

"The Morrigna. The Morrigna. The Morrigna comes!" chanted the birds.

Once again, I was swamped with guilt that I had put him in this position, but I stuffed that emotion down even as I was reaching blindly in my purse for my pepper spray. "Are those birds your mom?"

"It is the herald of the Morrigna. There. They have arrived."

"The Morrigna comes!" the ravens cawed.

They stopped a few yards away from us, just as the figures of two women appeared at the far end of the alley. The women started toward us, then paused for a moment. One of the two was Jerry, while the other was a dark-haired woman in a long black coat that moved gently around her, as if she were standing in a perpetual breeze.

Jerry stared to the side and made an abrupt gesture, obviously talking to someone else. The dark-haired woman put her hands on her hips as she, too, appeared to argue with someone out of our view.

"Should we run?" I asked Owain in a whisper.

"No," he said on a long, extremely martyred sigh. "I will have it out with her. Again. Stay back, out of the way in case she tries to bespell me again and decides you are collateral."

"Your mother put a spell on you?" I asked, horrified. "To do what?"

"Imprison me until I returned the boon she placed on me and my brothers. I wonder who she has as a third. She had the original third Morrigan killed last year." Owain glanced back at me when Jerry marched out of view, frowning when he noticed I had my phone out. "Are you calling someone?"

"No, Googling what Morrigans and Morrignas are. Ah." I looked up to the now obviously impatient dark-haired woman still at the far end of the alley, gesticulating wildly at what I assumed was Jerry. "It's three sisters who have something to do with war and kings. Your mom is part of that?"

"Yes. That's Badb," he said, indicating the dark-haired woman.

"Five?" I asked.

"No, the name is pronounced 'bive,' although Jerry says she has also adopted a more modern name. Ah. It is Macha my mother has roped into being a third member." He rolled his shoulders. "I will do what I can to keep you safe, but if they overpower me, get away. Find an Internet café, and don't leave it until you are sure they are not outside waiting for you."

"An Internet café? Why there?" I asked, and, for the second time that day, clutched my pepper spray prepared for a fight.

"Their father was a druid. As such, they have a natural aversion to anything that flies in the face of nature, including modern technology."

The ravens suddenly poured upward before spinning around behind us, effectively trapping us between them and the three women who were swiftly approaching.

"The Morrigna! The Morrigna!" the birds chanted again.

"Shut up!" I snarled at them, glaring over my shoulder. "We heard you the first time. Now, bugger off or we'll see how you like pepper spray up your schnozz … er … beak holes."

To my surprise, the ravens reeled back just as if they'd practiced the movement, their eyes spitting outrage at us. They didn't leave, but at least they stopped yakking, which I figured was a point in our favor.

The three women approaching appeared to be arguing.

"Right," I said, anger, guilt, and irritation sloshing around inside me at being the cause of trouble for what I firmly believed was a nice man, until, with no other option for resolution, I channeled it into action. "This is bullshit. I'm not going to stand here while your mom and her sisters and those freaking ravens who never shut up do something heinous to you."

"We stopped," one of the ravens protested behind me. "Not that you asked nicely. Would it have hurt you to ask instead of threatening us? We have feelings, you know."

The other ravens murmured agreement.

I slid a glance toward Owain. His martyred expression was back and firmly in place.

"I got you into this and I'm going to get you out," I told him. "Stay here."

I took five steps toward Jerry and her sisters before he realized what I was doing.

"Hey," I said as the women approached. "Your son is fine, but he's not going to be your prisoner again."

Owain was at my side by the time I was halfway through the sentence, his expression furious … at me.

"What the hell do you think you're doing?" he asked me.

"Fixing the problem I made for you. Now, shush," I said, taking another step forward so I was in front of him.

"You did not just hush me!" he said, outrage dripping from each word as he pulled me back to his side.

"What words of opposition do you dare speak to me?" Jerry seemed to snap her teeth together over the words, leaving me with the impression that she wanted to bite something, and I had a feeling it might be me. "I didn't ask you what he wants; he won't be free of me until he gives back what he holds, and if he's lucky, I won't smite him on the spot. Now, get out of my way lest I turn you into a bug."

"I shushed you," I told Owain, giving him a reassuring pat on the arm. "That's a gentler, kinder hush. Hang on, I got this."

"No, you do not," Owain growled, and tried again to stuff me behind him.

"Jerry, I need to tell you that I am armed, and if you make any hostile action toward Owain or me, I will defend us. The ravens are another matter. You can have at them all you want. Not that I condone any sort of animal abuse, but they have it coming."

"Hey!" the mouthy raven protested.

I ignored it, as well as their mutters that a group poop on me might be called for.

"You dare threaten me?" Jerry seemed to swell with rage. "You, a mere knocker, think to challenge me? I am the Morrigan!"

"Oh, lordy-loo." The woman who I figured was the one named Macha stopped and slapped her hands on her thighs. "This is ridiculous, Jerry. It's obvious that Owain is hale and hearty, although that mine ghost looks unhinged. She could do anything, and I'm wearing Miu Miu. I'm not risking that with a madwoman brandishing pepper spray. I'm going back to my Hour."

"Will you stop protecting me?" Owain asked, his brows pulled together. Even frowning, the man was drop-dead gorgeous. "Thank you. Now get behind me so that I may face my mother's wrath without any of it spilling onto you."

"Dammit! Stop reading my smutty thoughts about you," I told him, and refused to be shoved back. I gestured with my pepper spray toward the now two women. "I'm responsible for this situation, so I'm going to fix it. Let me do that, and then we'll talk about why you think it's OK to give me orders."

Jerry lunged at me at that moment, her fingernails like claws as she grabbed at me. Panicked, I leaped backward, at the same time my fingers tightened on the pepper spray, resulting in a stream of spray hitting her dead in the face. The woman named Badb caught the edge of the cone of liquid, both women immediately screaming, while Jerry went to her knees clutching her face.

"Blessed goddess!" I gasped when I realized what I'd done.

"Holy shit," one of the ravens said. "She took down the Morrigan. Right, that's us done."

The fluttering of wings faded behind us as I started forward, intending on helping Jerry. "I didn't mean to actually spray you. Here, let me wipe it off."

"You will do no such thing," Owain said, grabbing me by the arm and spinning me around. We were halfway down the alley before a second passed.

I tried to look over my shoulder, but Owain's legs were longer than mine, and I almost had to trot to keep up with him. "I didn't really want to pepper spray her," I explained.

"I know you didn't, but it's exactly what we needed to escape."

We emerged onto a busy street, Owain quickly surveying the situation, while I looked back. Badb was standing over her sister, who was still kneeling, rocking back and forth.

"It won't be safe to return to my flat, since my mother knows where I live. We will have to find accommodations elsewhere—who are you calling now?"

An unfortunate desire to giggle rose at the outrage in his voice, but I quelled it even as I tucked away the restaurant's business card, which I'd grabbed for future visits. "Calling the dragon people to have them help your mom and aunt. Hi, there are two pepper-sprayed … er … druids?" I hesitated, eyeing Owain as he decided on a direction, and more or less hauled me down the sidewalk.

"Celtic gods," Owain corrected.

I blinked a couple of times, having figured the part of Wikipedia I'd read about the Morrigan was referring to mythology, not real life, but duly repeated, "There are two Celtic gods in the alley behind your garden who need medical aid."

"Ah," the man who answered the phone said. "Do they? We will attend to them. Who is this? I ask merely so I may inform them of the name of their Good Samaritan."

"Yeah, I'm not really that," I admitted. "I'm the one who pepper sprayed them. Thanks so much!"

I hung up to the sound of the man sputtering.

"She will be fine in a few minutes," Owain said, lifting his hand when he spotted a taxi. "Gods, Celtic and otherwise, tend not to be overly affected by such things. Do you reside in London?"

"In the suburbs, yes," I answered, still feeling bad about inadvertently spraying Owain's mom and aunt. "Are you sure they'll be OK?"

"Yes. Does Jerry have your address?"

"I think so. Why? Do you think she'll come after me for attacking her?" I fretted with that thought, adding it to the woes that beset me.

"No, but if she knows where you live, it will not be safe for us to stay there. We'll find a hotel."

"I'm not going to a hotel with you," I said, refusing to get into the cab when it pulled up before us. "Your lower lip and jaw and hair aside, I don't go to hotels with men I've just met."

"You are in danger from my mother," Owain argued. "I can protect you from her taking vengeance upon you."

"A vengeance that is justified, although again, I feel compelled to say I truly did not intend to spray her. I wanted to threaten her so we could get away."

"Which is why you will come with me. I know you did not mean to harm her, but she will believe you have turned on her. She does not tolerate those she deems as traitors. Get in the cab so that we can find somewhere safe."

"I'm very good at apologies," I protested, refusing again to be pushed into the taxi. "Goddess knows I've had enough experience offering them. You go find a safe place where she can't find you, and I'll go back and apologize. And stop making that face. She can't hurt me, not really. I'm a knocker. I'm immortal."

He leaned close, his breath touching my cheek. "You may be immortal, but I assure you that you can be killed."

"Well, yes, strictly speaking, I guess that's true, but it would take someone of exceptional power. ..." My words slowed and came to an abrupt stop when I realized what I was saying.

Owain nodded. "Like a Celtic god. I don't wish to frighten you, but if she regains the boon she gave my brothers and me, I guarantee she'd not only be able to destroy you; she'd happily do so. She's a very vengeful person. Just ask any number of ancient kings of Ireland."

"Oy," I said, glancing worriedly toward the alley.

"Know this, Berengaria—"

"Berry, please," I interrupted. "Only my mom calls me by my full name."

"I assure you, Berry, if the Morrigna gets me alone, I don't know if I could hold out against them. Singularly, I can cope, but together, bound as the Morrigna ..." He shook his head. "Even my mother's boon wouldn't be enough to protect me."

I was about to protest when an enraged screech sounded behind us. We spun around to see Jerry stumbling down the block, long black lines of mascara dripping down her face, making her resemble something out of a horror movie. "You'll die for this outrage!" she swore, one hand beginning to draw the symbols of a spell.

"I've changed my mind," I said, and leaped into the taxi, pulling Owain in after me before instructing the driver, "Go!"

"Where?" he asked.

"Anywhere," Owain answered, watching through the window as the taxi headed into traffic. "Make it quick."

I thought hard for a minute, sent a text, and leaned forward to give the driver an address.

"If that's your flat—" Owain started to say.

"Not mine." I held my phone and sent a prayer that my plea would not reach a closed mind. "It's my cousin's house. We should be safe from your mom there. My cousin's wife is a dragon."

Owain said nothing as I sat back, but I swore I could feeling him thinking a good many things.

SIX
AISLING

"This is not the sort of place I expected Becket and Yrian to pick." I glanced around to make sure Ysolde and I weren't being overheard, and I snuggled a little deeper into my plush coat against the bitter cold. "For some reason, I pictured them in a modern house, all windows and glass and chrome. But this? Yes, it's very manor house, which also kinda fits Yrian's personality, although I didn't realize Wales had historic manor houses. I guess it makes sense they did, because they had nobles and peasants like the rest of Britain."

"It's the llama sanctuary," Ysolde said as she adjusted the white cashmere scarf that was wrapped around her head, neck, and lower face. "It almost makes me wish we hadn't left Anduin at your place."

"While I, on the other hand, am perfectly happy to take a break from all children," I answered, pulling the frosty air deep into my lungs. It was so cold, it felt like tiny icy daggers. "My ears are still buzzing after two days of constant shrieks, shouts, assorted yells, incredibly off-tune Christmas carols bellowed at an uncomfortably loud volume, and the nonstop chatter from fourteen excited children. Time spent with adults is a blessed relief."

Ysolde laughed. "You're the one who offered to have a two-day sleepover Christmas party for all the kids."

"It seemed like a good idea at the time," I said with a wry twist of my lips, turning when Jim left the men and headed our way. "And it let me check off reciprocal visits with you and Allie."

"Meh," Ysolde said, moving with me over to the side of the three-story, white stone, almost two-hundred-dred-year-old manor house that Becket and Yrian had purchased. They decorated it with enough lights to make Clark Griswold happy, including lights on the roof in the shape of a cat dressed as Santa. "You know you're welcome to visit us whenever without any sense of obligation. And I didn't mean I was angsting for Anduin's presence. … Like you, the last two days were exhausting, so a break is most welcome. Anduin was nigh on delirious with joy he got to stay for another day with what he's now calling his cousins, so I appreciate you letting him remain."

I couldn't help but smile at that. "My kids decided he and Brom are family, and no amount of explanation by Drake of how the septs work will convince them that your kids—and by extension the rest of the light dragons—aren't family."

"Uh-oh. It sounds like we've inadvertently stepped on Drake's toes," she said, a little frown forming between her brows.

"Not in the least," I said, waving when Becket emerged from the nearest end of the house, bearing a large tray loaded with mugs of what I hoped was hot mulled wine. We both turned to head her way. "I think it's more he wants them to understand the history of the green dragons, and it's a bit tricky when he has to avoid all the parts like wars and murders and such. Plus, it's good for our kids to embrace as family people who may not be related by blood, but should be, and you guys definitely are that."

"Aww," Ysolde said, pausing to give me a swift hug. "We consider all of you fam, as well. Baltic is certainly grateful that Drake is lending so many green dragons to help Brom with extra tutoring and weapon training. He—Baltic, not Brom—has been so busy helping Yrian get set up, financially and modern-life-wise, he hasn't had time to do much else. Thankfully, I think his turn at being his brother's keeper is over, and he can return to brooding about ways to annoy Kostya."

I laughed aloud at that before helping Becket unload her tray on a stone table that had been decorated with red and gold berries. "Hot wine or cocoa?" I asked, setting out the empty mugs while Ysolde took charge of two large insulated carafes.

"Both," Becket answered, turning when a woman emerged from the house holding two more trays, these filled with several small bowls and a stack of tasting plates. "Ayo thought we should have some peppermint cocoa to offset all the dragon's blood that Yrian has decided is necessary to show good hostiness. And we went a bit nuts with the snacks, since I told her how yummy the ones were that Allie and Ysolde had at their places."

"Did someone say snacks?" Jim, who had been out with the men while Yrian showed them the llama sanctuary that was part of the land they'd bought a few months before, made a beeline for the granite patio where we stood. "Oooh! Lots of good noms. I'll check a couple of those for you to make sure they're up to standards."

"You'll do nothing of the sort," I told Jim with a frown I knew it would ignore. I'd been a bit worried about it of late, and took a good look at it now to make sure it wasn't sinking into a decline. I knew it was worried about its parents, and their war on the Court of Divine Blood, so I leaned down to ask quietly, "Is anything upsetting you? Was it Cecile? I told you that as soon as she recovers from her dental work, Yrian agreed to bop her on the head and make her immortal."

It slid a glance up at me before rubbing its face on my leg. "Naw, I'm good there. And thanks for giving me the early Christmas present of paying for Yrian to do that. I want Cecile to live for all time with clean teeth, even if she is now missing a few of them."

"Yrian would have done it without charging us, but Drake insisted. I gather the money is going to llama care, so it's all to the good. If it's not Cecile that's worrying you, did your dad upset you?" I asked, knowing it had received a few texts from Desi, but since Jim hadn't shared what was being said, I felt a bit adrift. "Did they turn down the invitation to Boxing Day dinner? If they aren't comfortable coming to our place for that, we can meet them elsewhere. I bet we could convince Bastian to open up his restaurant if we needed it."

"Desi said they'd be there, and I don't think he'd lie about that," Jim said with a doggy shrug.

"Then what is it that's bothering you?" I asked, noting that the men, no doubt drawn by the lure of hot dragon's blood wine, were now marching across the frozen ground in a determined manner.

Allie, wife of Christian Dante, the head vampire of all the vampires in the world (or so I assumed—I made a mental note to ask Allie for clarification), emerged from the house clad in a dark-blue ankle-length coat, with matching fake-fur ushanka hat. "Sorry about having to take a phone call. The twins got in a swivet because they thought they lost their phones, but our nanny felt it only right that the girls' phones be taken away during your children's no-screen time, Aisling. That's an excellent policy, by the way, and I think Christian and I will gradually introduce the same into our lives. Despite my children's moans to the contrary, a little time without phones and tablets isn't going to end in their demise. Oh, that looks so yummy, Becket. What a fun idea to have an outdoor picnic. That firepit is perfect for keeping away the cold. Can I help with anything?"

Becket murmured something about having everything well in hand as I cast a raised eyebrow at Jim, moving a few steps away to wrap up our conversation.

It gave a dramatic sigh, then said softly, "It's Lattsa."

"Your half sister?" I shot a worried look over to where Drake was approaching. "Is she still trying to guilt you into helping your parents take down the Court of Divine Blood?"

"No." It was silent for a moment, then said in a bit of a rush, "It's a feeling I have that something's not right with her. Not like she's batshit crazy or anything, although I suppose she could be, because she's into old earth magic and stuff, but something about her helping Desi doesn't fit."

"Doesn't fit how?" I asked. Drake was about twenty yards away and approaching fast, his gaze now locked onto me. While I would never keep anything from him that might endanger our family, the sept, or any of our friends, he had less tolerance for dealings with Jim's parents than I thought prudent.

It gave another shrug. "Dunno. There's just something off."

"Let me know if she says anything to you, or if you get a better sense of what's wrong," I told it, patting it on the head as I turned to face the love of my life. Even now, the liquid heat in his emerald eyes made my bones turn to jelly. "I'm glad you made it back in time to enjoy all the food and hot dragon's blood. I take it all is well with the llamas?"

Drake's lips curled slightly, handing me a mug of dragon's blood before taking one for himself. The other wyverns had gathered around, as well, taking up the spicy beverage that pretty much only dragons could drink without suffering dire consequences. "The only thing that kept me from being bored was watching Baltic trying to appear interested while his brother explained the running of the sanctuary."

I gave a soft laugh, careful not to catch anyone's attention as I watched Ysolde fuss over Baltic, no doubt sensing he was about at the end of his not-substantial patience. "I bet that was a sight to see."

Becket finished pouring hot wine from one of the carafes before saying, "I know you guys like to have your fight-club thing before snacks, but since there's only four of you, Yrian had a great idea for something fun as an alternative. We've set up one of the barns for a starlight beatdown."

"Sporting," Yrian corrected, one arm around her, making me smile to myself. I leaned into Drake's side, pleased that Becket and Yrian had found each other. It was a bit uncanny how much Yrian looked like his dad, the progenitor of all dragons, but the former's personality was definitely all his own, and much quirkier than that of the First Dragon. "The word is 'sporting.' We will have starlight sporting where lights will be at a minimum. There are some beams wrapped with padding so as to avoid serious injury, and occasional laser lights to confuse and distract. We can make two teams of two, or I suggest going solo."

"Oooh, laser tag dragon-style?" Jim said, snuffling one of the plates that was a bit too close to the edge of the table. I nudged my furry demon with my knee. It rolled its eyes in response. "Can I play, too?"

All the dragons considered Jim. Yrian moved off without a comment, heading for where Christian stood at the edge of the patio.

"I wouldn't want you getting hurt," I told Jim, hesitant to ruin something it might find fun.

"Eh," it answered with a bit of its old cocky grin. "They'd have to catch me to do that."

I looked at Drake. He thought for a few seconds, then said, "With the changes Yrian has arranged due to our numbers, I do not see a problem if Jim wishes to join, but I would remind it that dragons can be very fast when we so desire."

It wasn't the way he said it, but the fact that he cracked his knuckles while doing so, that had me stifling another laugh.

Jim, knowing full well that Drake would never harm it, curled a lip at him. "Yeah, yeah, but do you know how fast a demon in fear of its magnificent coat can move? Faster than any dragon in human skin."

"And that's enough with the trash-talking each other," I said, stopping Drake before he could respond. "The evening event sounds like fun, Becket, and I'm sure everyone will enjoy it. Do we get to watch?"

"Yup. We decorated the entire barn for the holidays, so the pillars are wrapped like candy canes, and there are foam truncheons in the shape of festive gnomes. Yrian is particularly looking forward to dual wielding gnomes against his brother." Becket turned when Christian, who had his phone out and was consulting with Yrian, hurried over to where the rest of us were clustered.

He stopped next to Allie, his silver eyes glittering with what I assumed was excitement.

"I am pleased to tell you all that I've received word from Finch that he and Tatiana have not only returned to the mortal world, but their lives have been restored."

"Whoa," Ysolde said, a crab-and-cheese-stuffed mini pepper halfway to her mouth. "How did they pull off that miracle?"

"They were removed from the Hour by its previous lord," Christian answered, moving aside when Allie reached for white cheddar and apple *gougères* that instantly had me salivating.

"That sounds both annoying in that they set the place up the way they wanted and then got the boot, but on the other hand ... yeah. Life and back to reality. That's hard to beat." I took a second Parmesan and pesto twist, since I'd gobbled down the first, broke up into smaller chunks one of the plain cheese twists that Becket had made for Jim, and placed it on the plate it was happily cleaning.

We spent a pleasant (if nippy on the nose despite the roaring fire in the pit) ten minutes while Finch and Tatiana's recent adventure was recounted.

"And I have further good news," Christian said, bowing his head to Yrian. "They will be joining us shortly, thanks to Yrian's invitation, and a portal shop in Cardiff."

Becket froze midway through chewing a small thumbprint chorizo pizza, her eyes calculating. "Of course your nephew and his wife are welcome." Her gaze met that of Yrian for a few seconds. "Thank god we had all the bedrooms renovated when we did the rest of the house. I'll go mention it to Ayo and will check that the yellow room has linens on the bed."

My phone dinged at me when she hustled into the house. "May is calling. No doubt to see if we all survived two days of excited children hopped-up on sugar. Hello, May." I moved off a short distance in order to speak with her.

"Are you at Becket's place?" she asked, her voice sounding both excited and breathless, as if she was running while speaking.

"Yes, we're all here. Well, all as in Ysolde and Baltic, and Allie and Christian. Evidently, Christian's nephew Finch and his wife are on the way, as well. They're out of their Hour."

"Oh, good, that's going to make things so much easier. No, I gave the passports to Maata. Should I close up the safe?"

I gathered from the male rumble barely audible in my phone, and the fact that May was obviously speaking to someone else, that Gabriel was with her.

"Are you guys leaving? I thought you were spending Christmas with Kawaa and your nieces?"

"We are. We will. But we're heading to the airport to fly to England. I hate to be so fast, but we're in a rush to close up the house since Maata and Tipene are coming with us. We've heard from Savian."

"OK," I said, not sure what had her and Gabriel in such a fuss, but a cold, clammy feeling started to grow in my stomach. "Is something wrong? Should I warn Drake?"

"Gabriel is texting the wyverns as soon as we are in the car," she said, now definitely short of breath. She murmured something about that being the last of the luggage. "Savian called to wish us a happy holiday, and to thank us for the presents for him and Maura and the kids, and mentioned that his cousin has taken on the job of thief taker for Dr. Kostich. Oh, coats!"

"Coats to you, too," I said, half startled, and more than a little confused.

"Gabriel, we need coats! It's cold in England now. Aisling, apologize for me to Becket for foisting two more people on her, but there really was nothing else to be done. Where? Oh, hell's bells. No, I'll get them."

"You mean Finch and Tatiana?" I asked, turning to look back at everyone. "I think that's cool with Yrian and Becket."

"No, Savian's cousin. Sorry, I know I'm being incoherent, but there's a storm rolling in, and we're trying to get to Gabriel's shiny new plane before we get grounded for a few hours. Savian's cousin Berry is a thief taker, and she was hired by the vampire thanes' mom to find him. The guy who Finch let out of the Hour. The dangerous guy that Christian and all the vampires are worried about."

"Holy *merde*," I said, my eyebrows rising as I tried to piece together her explanation. "So, this cousin is coming here? Did she find the thane?"

"Yes, he's with her. From what Savian said, he's not evil, but they are being pursued, and worse, they are insisting they get Desi's blood moon."

"Oh, lord," I said, smiling broadly at Drake when he cocked an inquisitive eyebrow at me.

Unfortunately, our time together gave the man annoyingly accurate perception into my attempts to defuse his suspicions, and he instantly set down his plate of snacks and started toward me.

"Gabriel says we need to be there to help the weyr with the thane, since we promised to help Christian, as well as a feeling he says he has that the thane has something to do with the dragons. And before you ask, he doesn't know what, exactly—he just says it's a feeling that's getting stronger each day. Ready? Yes, I have everyone's coats." Murmured voices and the thumping of car doors told me the silver dragons were on the move. "I'm going to hop off the call, Aisling. Gabriel is texting the wyverns now. We should be in England sometime tomorrow afternoon. If we're needed sooner, let me know and we'll stop somewhere and take a portal."

Drake, about ten feet from me, paused when his phone pinged, followed shortly by Baltic's and Yrian's phones also alerting them to an incoming text.

"Christian, I think I have potentially some more good news for you vampires," I said, tucking away my phone as the men simultaneously looked up from their respective phones and over to him.

"Dark Ones," he corrected automatically, looking curious. "What news is it you have?"

"May says Savian Bartholomew's cousin—he's a thief taker, now married to a dragon—is on her way here with your missing thane."

"What?" The word shot out of him with the velocity of a bullet. "How is this possible?"

"Holy cow," Allie said, tucking her hand into Christian's. "Is he OK? Is the cousin OK? How did she find him?"

"According to Gabriel, the thane's mother hired her." Drake read out the pertinent points from Gabriel's text as Becket returned from domestic duties.

"Is the room with the blue flowers still available?" Yrian asked her.

"The small one? Yes, although I didn't finish decorating in there, so it's just the basic furniture. Why?" she asked, her expression turning to one of suspicion. "Don't tell me someone else is staying?"

We briefly explained the situation while Christian sent what I assumed were texts to his people.

"Sure, another demigod will be fun to have around the house," Becket said when we finished taking turns filling her in. Her voice was rich with irony, although I thought she was secretly amused by the situation.

"I don't know that he's all that. I mean, if he was a demigod, he probably could have gotten himself out of the Seventh Hour—" I started to say, but Jim snorted at the same time Yrian shook his head.

"Thanes are not demigods, but they are similar in nature. They simply draw their abilities from mortal beings rather than the elements, as we do," he said, his expression thoughtful. "I believe I met one of them in battle, although I have little memory of our interaction. Regardless, we have sworn to aid you with your thane, Christian, so it is good he is coming here, where we may subdue him if he is not as the silver wyvern claims."

"Good lord, is that them already?" Ysolde asked, shielding her eyes against the frosty sunlight, watching as an SUV appeared at the top of a hill to the north, dipping down as the road headed into the small valley in which the farm was located. She asked Baltic, "Should we do something to meet the thane? You have the light sword with you, yes?"

"Gabriel may be many things, but he has yet to prove himself a bad judge of character," Baltic answered somewhat cryptically, and also, I noticed, ignoring Ysolde's question about whether he had a magic sword concealed somewhere about his person. "If he says the thane is not a threat, then I don't see we need to protect ourselves beyond normal measures."

"I think that's Finch and Tat," Allie said, leaning into Christian to read his phone. "Yes, they texted that they see the farm."

We moved into the warmth of the big house once Finch had arrived, and introductions were made all around.

"I don't know about all this," I said from in front of a massive stone fireplace. Ysolde and Allie were with me as we warmed our butts while watching the interaction of the others. Becket had taken Tatiana upstairs with their luggage while Finch remained in close consultation with his uncle and the wyverns. "Something seems …"

"Off?" Allie asked, shooting a glance at her husband. "Christian basically just said the same thing. Our Horsemen—the vamps' version of the Watch—are insisting they portal out here immediately so they can help Christian, but I don't think he's really worried about that."

"I'm with him, there," I said, rubbing my arms, feeling chilled even though the house was warm and comfy. "It feels like something that looks one way is really another."

"Something?" Ysolde asked, shifting to the side when Becket and Tatiana returned. Becket stayed with us while Tatiana peeled off to join Finch. "A person, place, or thing?"

"I don't know." I studied Jim for a few seconds. It was flaked out on the dog bed I brought with us when we went visiting, but it was clearly listening to the men as they spoke. I had a feeling Jim knew more than it was telling me. "I wish I could pin it down, but I can't."

"I can't help but think that every time we seem to come to an easy resolution of a problem, things get worse," Ysolde commented. "It all started with Xavier and the bad dragons, then Bael and his crazy mom, and now Jim's dad is insisting we locate and give him a majorly powerful relic."

"I share that feeling," I said, and would have tried to pinpoint the origin of the worry that seemed to prickle along my skin, but at that moment, the sound of a car arriving could be heard, and everyone turned to look out the large windows at the parking area.

"Thane incoming," I said, and gestured Jim over to my side. If this Owain person thought he could fool us, I'd be ready.

SEVEN
OWAIN

"You must return to the Hour!"

Owain considered the men who stood before him, two Dark Ones, both furious, and both, he felt, about at their wit's end. He didn't wonder at that, since he, too, was done with all this foolishness.

"I don't suppose you know any spells to grant insight, do you?" he asked Berry.

Her nose wrinkled while she thought. Owain had never been an admirer of nose-wrinkling in the past, but it was a charmingly adorable look when Berry did it. Sexy, almost. His libido certainly felt the last was accurate, and once again, an erection threatened to ensue if he kept admiring her oval face, her silky black hair, and the greenish brown of her eyes that reminded him of autumn leaves lying in a shallow stream.

He really enjoyed looking at all her other bits, but mindful of her rejection of his offer of lovemaking the night before, when they were squished together into a child's room at her cousin's house, he managed to keep from admiring her plentiful curves.

His hands practically itched with the need to caress those curves.

"Owain?"

He was called out of his lustful thoughts by Berry's voice, and the pointed look she gave him that warned he'd been asked a question. "My apologies, I was distracted. I will not return to the Hour, as I've said four times now."

"You have to," the Dark One named Finch said, making a sharp gesture. "It's dangerous for you to be out."

"How so?" he asked, his attention immediately moving to Berry when she shifted next to him. Her nickname certainly fit her, since she was as ripe and sweet as a sun-warmed strawberry.

"You are a danger to the mortal world," Finch insisted, while the one who'd been introduced as Christian Dante stood silent, his gaze assessing. "You'll destroy it in your attempt to seek revenge. Tatiana and I are tangentially responsible for your release, so you'll understand when we tell you it's important you return to the Hour so no mortals will perish in the name of revenge."

Owain thought about what the Dark One said, before turning to Berry. "They seem to think we wish to harm mortals."

"They're wrong," she said, shifting again until she was almost touching him, the gesture not only warming his heart but firing his libido even higher. "You're doing everything to keep from hurting people."

"I am," he agreed, then, unable to keep the question to himself, asked, "When you said no to lovemaking last night because we were at your cousin's house, did that mean that you would be happy to do so elsewhere?"

She shot him a look that by rights should have scorched the hair from his head. It made him want to laugh, that and the furious way she scrambled to hide the thoughts she had regarding him, his body, and all the things she wanted to do to him. "Dude! Now is not the time to discuss mutual itch scratching."

"I don't believe scratching was in the top ten items on your list of things you wished to do to me," he said, delighted with the way emotion made her eyes glint. She was an intriguing woman, clearly wasted on the job of hunting individuals. A vision arose in his mind of her riding across a grassy plain, her black hair streaming behind her like a silk banner, mortals scattering before the pounding hooves of her mount. He paused at that thought, then added, "Perhaps I am not as blameless as I thought I was, since your horse would definitely trample mortals."

"What horse?" she asked, her eyes going a little wild. "What mortals?"

"The ones in my mental vision of you." He turned to where the two Dark Ones were now standing silent, watching them.

At the far end of the room, several dragons were clustered, ostensibly sitting around a fireplace, but he knew the focus of all was on Berry and him. "Why do you believe I am a danger to mortals? Have you spoken to my mother? She is not to be trusted, not when it comes to my brothers and me. She has what they call issues."

The two men exchanged glances before Christian said slowly, "You swore vengeance against all who aided in your downfall, including the mortals who turned their backs on you in your time of need, and the Dark Ones who resulted from the curse. For that reason, we ask that you return to the Hour, so that no one will be further harmed."

"That's ridiculous," Berry said, her hand brushing against his. He realized from a thought she tried to keep hidden that she wanted him to hold it, and accordingly did so.

Her hand felt right in his, her fingers curling in a manner that had him once again at war with his libido.

"Owain isn't evil. He said some of his brothers are, but Owain doesn't want to hurt anyone, do you?" Berry turned to him, her mysterious eye glints now speaking volumes of her righteous indignation.

It warmed him to the spot where his soul used to reside that someone was indignant on his behalf.

"I wouldn't mind squashing a few demon lords," he admitted, for a handful of seconds dwelling with much pleasure on what he'd like to do to Desislav for his part in the thanes' imprisonment. "But on the whole, I do not seek revenge. Not even toward my mother, who I now believe is downright delusional in her quest to regain access to the Celtic Pantheon."

"The what, now?" Berry asked. "A pantheon? Is that what you were going to discuss last night before you suddenly appeared stark naked and asked if I wanted to hook up?"

Both Dark Ones eyed him with unreadable expressions.

"That was because you kept thinking things about my hair and chest and arms, although I don't understand the term 'hip-hop' in relation to my hair. That aside, I assumed you wished to explore a sexual relationship," he answered, a bit testily, to be true.

She slid a glance toward the Dark Ones, lifting her chin as she said, "I don't know why you'd believe that."

"Why? Because you were thinking the most lascivious things possible about me. I assumed you wish to act on the attraction we both feel," he said.

"I never thought anything remotely smutty about you!" she declared, her eyes now filled with a mixture of irritation and arousal.

Her pupils dilated slightly when he raised his eyebrows at her statement.

"Fine," she just about snarled, shooting an indignant glance at the two Dark Ones. "I may have had a few stray thoughts about how nice you smell, but that's it."

"You also thought many things about my hair, and what you'd like to do to it," he reminded her. "Specifically, where you'd like it to touch you."

Both Dark Ones studied his hair.

"Oh!" Berry said, rounding on him, looking like she wanted to punch his nose. "You take that back! I thought about your hair brushing across my nipples earlier *yesterday*, when we were at that restaurant, not after we were at my cousin's house!"

The Dark One named Finch tipped his head toward Berry when he asked the other, "Beloved?"

His uncle looked thoughtful, then nodded. "I believe so."

"I am a thane, not a Dark One," he told them. "We do not have Beloveds."

"Well, bully for you," Berry said, actually whapping him on the arm, her eyes still glittering with ire and arousal. "Not that I care what you call a girlfriend, because I am not she. Her. Whatever is grammatically correct—I'm too annoyed to care. Not only that, I'd like to point out, Mr. Chatty Pants, that a gentleman doesn't kiss and tell to strangers."

"We haven't kissed," he pointed out. "Despite you wanting to suck on my lower lip. Would you like to do that now?"

She looked more outraged, if possible, which delighted him more.

"As a matter of fact, I would," she answered, taking him by surprise, which pushed his admiration of her quirky nature even higher.

With a defiant glance at the Dark Ones, she leaned into him, her breath brushing his lips as she started to scatter the softest kisses imaginable along his lips.

"What are you doing?" he asked a full minute later, when she stopped, a mixture of puzzlement and annoyance visible in her expression.

"Kissing you."

"Ah." He lifted an eyebrow a minute amount. "Would you like me to kiss you back? Although I'm not sure the idea of me starting at your knees and working my way up is appropriate in present company."

"Will you stop reading my thoughts!" she bellowed, catching the attention of everyone in the large hall. "It's rude, and besides, my brain thinks things about you that I didn't authorize, like the kissing my thighs and belly and … and … other parts."

"Definitely a Beloved," Finch told Christian, who looked thoughtful.

"Is that a yes or no to me kissing you in a manner appropriate to our surroundings?" he asked, squelching the bubble of laughter that wanted to rise in response.

It was enough of a struggle to keep a tight rein on his libido so that the dragons and Dark Ones didn't witness him sporting a full erection triggered by Berry, and he couldn't do that if he was too busy being amused.

"No," she said, giving an abrupt jerk of her head. "I don't want to kiss you anymore."

He raised his eyebrow a little higher.

She snarled something rude under her breath. "Later. You can return the kiss later. When everyone isn't staring at us like we're insects pinned to a board."

The dragons had re-formed their huddle. The two Dark Ones looked pained, as if they were both trying hard not to laugh at the ridiculous situation.

Owain knew how they felt.

"And my point still stands—it's not polite to tell strangers about intimate situations." She looked so self-righteous he wanted to give in and kiss her the way his body had been demanding since he first saw her standing at the entrance to Abaddon.

"Technically, they are family," he said, pointing to the two men before asking Christian, "Do you know which of the four of us you are descended from?"

"No," he answered, his expression changing quickly from surprise at the question to speculation. "But it is something I now wish to determine. The Moravian Council archives are seldom consulted, but I believe your return to the mortal realm gives us a good reason to go through the documents we have."

"I will help you as best I can," Owain promised.

The men hesitated, sending each other glances filled with meaning.

Owain sighed, and retaking the hand that Berry had snatched from him when she tried to downplay the attraction between them, he said, "Our attempt to remove evil from the world was born of good intentions, but the centuries I've spent imprisoned in the Hour has led me to realize such an outcome would never have worked. There must be darkness in order to have light, and to extinguish one would doom the other. I do not seek revenge against anyone, not even Desislav, although I can't allow him to regain the blood moon. Since it is not safe for the relic to be at large, I will devote myself to locating it, and removing it from Desi's sphere of influence."

"And that is where we have a problem," the dragon named Yrian said as he strode over to them, followed by the woman introduced as Finch's Beloved. "The dragonkin have need of the blood moon. I must use it to make changes in the weyr, and to stop my mother from rescuing my brother Kashi."

Owain eyed Yrian. He hadn't had time at their arrival to do more than note that the dragons had a demigod in their midst, and that Yrian had a golden aura that made Owain feel as if he were standing in direct sunlight.

He took a step backward, as did the two Dark Ones.

For a moment, something flared in Yrian's eyes.

"We mean no disrespect," Owain said, feeling it would be best not to anger his host. "Your aura affects us in a not pleasant manner."

"His aura?" Berry asked, her attention now on Yrian. "He has an aura? I don't see anything."

"That's because you are not a grandson of the druid Cailitin," Owain told her.

"Ah." Yrian's gaze shifted to that of Christian. "Is that why you backed away from me when we were at your castle?"

"I didn't realize you had an aura, as I am also not the grandson of a famed druid," Christian answered. "But as I am apparently his descendant, then yes, I could feel heat radiating from you, and it grew to be quite intense when you were near. I simply assumed it was an artifact of you being the son of a fire fury rather than something to do with your dragon nature."

"A fire fury would explain some of it, but not all," Owain said, now also studying Yrian. The latter's mate—Becket—and the other dragons joined them.

"He's also the firstborn son of the First Dragon," Becket said, giving Owain a warm smile. "That might account for the gold part of it."

"It seems to me we are at an impasse," Owain said, considering the dragons. "I have no animosity with your kind, but should you seek to keep the blood moon from me or, worse, to use it against me, I will be forced to take action."

The dragons didn't like that, and he could sense them closing ranks against him. To his surprise, the two Dark Ones didn't ally themselves with the dragons, but instead shifted subtly to indicate their allegiance lay with him.

"For Pete's sake, why is everyone suddenly going to war against us?" one of the female dragons asked, glaring at her dragon, who had exceptionally green eyes. "I'm not going through this stupid cycle of dancing around war with other beings, not again. We are older and wiser, and more importantly, we have children now. I'm not putting them at risk for a power struggle over a ridiculous relic! If you guys can't figure out how to work things out, we mates will."

Her dragon looked mildly shocked. "*Kincsem,*" he said, frowning at her. "The relic is anything but ridiculous. And we do not wish for war, but we will protect the kin against threats, just as the Dark Ones wish to protect their people."

"Pfft," one of the other mates, this one a blonde, said as she pushed past the dragon to stand next to the first female. In addition, she shot an indignant look around at the rest of them, the Dark Ones and Owain included. "Damn straight, Aisling. Baltic and I don't mind helping Yrian get back on his feet and find his place in the modern world, but Bael is well and truly out of our hair, and frankly, I'd like it to stay that way. If we get the blood moon, you'll mess around with his imprisonment, and then somehow, he'll miraculously escape again, and we'll be back to the start of this whole mess."

"Brava, Ysolde," Becket told her, applauding lightly, also now standing with the other two dragon mates. "I may not have kids, but as someone who *really* doesn't want Bael to get out of the Thirteenth Hour, I'm with you on the whole let sleeping murderous whoresons lie."

Everyone looked in surprise at her.

She cleared her throat and shot the demigod a tiny smile, adding, "Sorry, Yrian referred to him by that sobriquet a few days ago, and I thought it was fitting. Name-calling Bael aside, I don't see that you *need* to have the blood moon."

She'd spoken the last sentence to Yrian, who answered, "You forget that without it, I can't change the weyr. I have sworn to do so, and I will not forswear myself. Not to anyone, and especially not to kin."

"Yeah, but do you really have to do that?" The woman who spoke was the Beloved of Finch. Owain narrowed his gaze on her.

"What do you mean?" Finch asked; then suddenly his eyebrows rose. "Ah. That is a good point." His gaze shifted to Owain.

"Seriously, can we look into being able to do the mind talking that the vamps can do?" The dark haired mate asked the blonde. "Because it would be the end to so many arguments if we could know what each other was thinking."

"You'd think so," the woman named Allie said, leaning into her Dark One, who shot her a look tinged with amusement. "But sadly, we just argue in each other's heads rather than aloud. But I admit I'm curious as to what Tatiana meant, as well."

Tatiana nodded toward Yrian. "Well, it seems to me that of everyone who wants this blood moon thingie, the dragons have the best reasons to claim it. Aisling's demon's parents aside, and I assume no one wants *them* to have it back."

"Under no circumstances," Owain said firmly. "Desi would simply send me back to the Hour in which I've spent almost two thousand years confined."

A pregnant silence fell around them. To Owain's surprise—and pleasure—Berry took umbrage at the looks the others were passing around.

"No!" she said in a shout that had the male dragons taking a protective step toward their respective mates. "You guys can stop thinking that it wouldn't be so bad if Owain got shoved back in that Hour. For one, he hasn't done anything wrong, and for another, he and his brothers were cursed by Desislav and the other demon lords. He didn't deserve to have some blood curse bound onto him, and he certainly doesn't deserve to be punished for whackadoodle demon lords!"

"If you are making the case that all the thanes be released—" Finch started to say, but Owain stopped Berry before she could respond.

"Under no circumstances should Rhain and Rhys be released," he told them all. "Cadell doesn't seem to me to be a threat, so I suppose he could be out in the mortal world without issue, but not the other two."

"Yeah, Deacon—or, rather, Cadell—isn't quite the poster child for mental stability that you seem to think he is," Tatiana said, glancing at her Dark One. "For one, he hired a demon to kill his aunt, which admittedly was on his mom's order, but still. And then he was obsessed with making sacrifices to bring forth some old god."

"Which one?" Owain asked, momentarily distracted.

"We never found out," Finch said. "But Tatiana is correct that Cadell in the mortal world is ill-advised. I think we'd all be happier—and the world safer—if the thanes remained where they are. Now that Troy is back in charge, they won't be able to escape."

"OK, so both dragons and Owain have a need for the relic. My question is, why can't you guys share it?" Berry asked, her fingers finding his again. He took much pleasure in the fact that she liked to touch him. He very much wanted to explore touching her in return, but told himself now was not the time to discuss their future. First, he had to find the blood moon.

"Share it?" The blonde Ysolde looked at her dragon, who raised his eyebrows in thought. "You mean take turns using it?"

"What an excellent suggestion," the green dragon's mate said, nudging her dragon in the ribs. "That would solve everyone's problems, don't you think?"

"Far from it," the wyvern said, his gaze on Yrian.

"Who would hold it when it was not being used?" the light dragon asked.

"Once it was known it had been found, it would be the focus of many beings," Yrian said, frowning at nothing. "Tenite has offered a great price for news of its location."

"Tenite?" Owain asked, unfamiliar with the name.

"My mother," Yrian said with a grimace.

"She has serious anger-management issues," Becket said, her gaze dropping to her dragon's chest. "And not someone you want to mess with unless you have a bunch of asbestos blankets."

"Every thief taker and mercenary is out looking for the relic at Tenite's behest," Yrian added, his expression grim.

"Not *every* thief taker," Berry said, giving Owain a shy smile that he felt down to the tips of his toes.

"The point remains that passing the object between Dark Ones and dragons is not viable at all." The green-eyed dragon looked almost as fed up as Owain felt. "While we can see that Owain does not wish to return to the Hour—and frankly, given his statement that he means no ill toward mortals or Dark Ones, I don't see why he should be forced to do so—we cannot allow the blood moon to pass out of our protection once we regain it."

Owain considered the people in front of him, realized that discussion was not going to provide a solution, and, tightening his hold on Berry's hand, told her, "This is pointless. We will come to no agreement here. We will leave so that we might track down the blood moon ourselves."

"Now, hold on," Becket said when Owain started to leave. "We aren't done discussing this issue with you."

"We, on the other hand, are quite done talking in circles," Owain said, Berry next to him, but reluctantly, casting glances back at the others as he marched her past them.

"You know," Ysolde said to the curly-haired Aisling, "now might be a good time to let the boys get down and dirty. I suspect they could all use a little steam-letting, and I'm willing to bet that Owain would benefit from it, as well."

"I think that's an excellent idea, although it's not the midnight session we planned for," Becket said.

Berry stopped, effectively halting him, too. He gave a little tug to her hand. She fired her glittering eyes at him for a few seconds before turning back to the women and asking, "What do you mean, steam-letting?"

"We let the men beat the tar out of each other when they get testy," Ysolde answered, smiling brightly. "It sounds horrible, but I assure you, the men all look forward to it. We limit them to fighting with fists, so no one gets terribly hurt."

"You guys box each other?" Berry asked, both horrified and intrigued. He was a little surprised to find how intrigued she was by the idea of him fighting the dragons.

"Kind of, but with no gloves. No dragon claws, no vampire fangs, and no godly powers," Aisling answered.

Owain shifted his gaze to Christian, who made a wry face for a few seconds before admitting, "We have found it to be useful in the release of tension."

"Oh, you love joining the fray, and we all know it," Allie said with a smile shared with the other women. "Because there's only a few of the men present, Becket and Yrian set up a special space for the guys to duke it out. I know they would have loved doing it at night, but maybe now would be a better time to get rid of some of the animosity, so we can all talk later, when feelings aren't running so high."

Berry looked at him, her eyes searching his, but for what, he wasn't quite sure. Perhaps it was assessing his mental state, but she smiled again, and once again he felt as if he'd been standing in the full sunlight. "What do you think? Are you up to taking on a couple of drag-ons and vamps?"

"Dark Ones," both Finch and Christian murmured.

"Would you enjoy it if I was to participate?" he asked her, feeling a sudden, and unquenchable, need to show her his fighting prowess. "My grandsire taught my brothers and me well in the arts of warring, so I am not opposed if it would please you."

"The urge to say 'those are fighting words' is strong, but since I'm not the one doing the beatdown, I'll keep quiet," Aisling said to Ysolde.

"Trust us on this," Ysolde told Berry, taking her by the arm in order to lead her away from him. "It's great fun."

The females left together en masse, all of them but Tatiana reassuring Berry that while it sounded like something out of a Quentin Tarantino movie, it was actually beneficial to everyone involved.

Owain, watching as the dragons filed out after them, turned to Christian. "*Is* it beneficial?"

Finch gave a brief laugh, then strolled after the women.

"For Dark Ones?" Christian hesitated, then gave a quick smile. "Not really. It's been my experience that the dragons are much more volatile, emotionally speak-ing. Dark Ones have better regulation over our emo-tions, but I will admit that there is something satisfying about their style of fighting. I am not often afforded opportunities to indulge in such, and the dragons are excellent opponents."

"I suppose it is no different to using a punching bag," Owain said, falling into step alongside Christian as they left the house and followed the others to a large structure resembling a barn. "The lord of our Hour provided Rhain one when he kept breaking down the walls of the stable whenever he'd go into a rage. I will participate, but after that, we will leave. I can't allow the dragons to possess that which could mean my incarceration."

Christian was silent for ten steps before he answered, "If it comes down to that, we will naturally support your claim. I cannot help but hope, however, that we are able to regain the relic without disturbing the dragonkin, especially Yrian. He has a great deal more power than is apparent, and I would not relish going against him."

Owain's gaze went to the man in question, a slow smile curling his lips.

He might not be a dragon demigod, but he was a thane.

It would be enough.

EIGHT
BERRY

"I can't find a delicate way to ask this, so I'm going to come right out with it." The redheaded Becket gave me an apologetic half smile. Her voice had a tone that was particularly lyrical, making me sigh to myself about my own voice, which a former boyfriend once kindly referred to as smoky. "Are you with Owain? That is, are you OK with sharing a bedroom? If you aren't, I'm sure we can bed him down on a couch somewhere."

I wanted to say that I would prefer if he slept elsewhere, but the memory of the hours I'd spent the previous night being hyperaware of Owain on the bottom of Savian's kids' bunk beds remained high in my mind.

"I don't want to put you to any more trouble than we are, so it's fine if he stays in a room with me," I answered, well aware that it had taken every morsel of self-control that I possessed to turn down a stark naked Owain offering to pleasure me, and I wasn't sure I could manage it again.

Not while an oddly overwhelming protective surge swamped me at the knowledge that the dragons didn't give a damn about him … and I wasn't overly certain about the two vampires.

"We have only ourselves to rely on," I murmured to myself as I walked across frozen ground to a barn.

"Really?" The woman introduced as Ysolde stopped about a dozen paces in front of us and turned with a pointed look directed at me.

"Dragons have very good hearing," Aisling said as she passed by with a demon in dog form, whose presence no one seemed inclined to explain. "Jim, if you have something helpful to impart, you may speak."

"Hoo, baby," the demon said, walking next to me. "Heya, Berry, is it? Name's Jim. Effrijim, really, but no one calls me that but Desi and Parisi. So, you're a knocker turned thief taker? How's that working out?"

"Desi as in Desislav?" I asked, wondering what on earth I was doing talking to a demon.

"Yup. He's my dad. Parisi used to be Sovereign. She's my mom, although she doesn't remember that, because she went into the Beyond to keep from dying after I was born, and peeps left her in there for so long, she lost her memory."

"You're Desislav's *son*?" I asked, horror crawling down my flesh. I shot a desperate glance toward Owain, at the entrance of the barn. He immediately spun around, his eyes narrowing on the demon.

"Yeah, but it's cool. I live with Ash and Drake and their spawn, and Desi promised they won't try to off them. Well, unless they don't give him the blood moon, but I doubt he's serious about wiping out dragons if we don't." Jim pursed its doggy lips before adding, "Then again, they've got their hearts set on taking down the Court, and I don't see how they're going to do that without the blood moon. Still, you gotta have hope, right?"

Owain's eyes went almost black as the pupils dilated, this time with pure, unadulterated rage. He snarled something in what sounded to me like Latin, making an odd symbol in the air, and poof! Suddenly the demon dog was gone.

"Jim!" Aisling spun around, her face frozen for a few seconds before she started toward Owain. "What the hell did you do to it?"

The dragons turned at her words, and I didn't like their expressions at all. I dropped polite pretense and hurried to Owain's side, bracing myself for trouble.

"I sent it to the Akasha," he told Aisling, his demeanor and voice calm, but I could feel anger roiling around inside him. "It is the son of Desislav, and will tell him of our plans. I cannot allow that."

"What you can't do is banish my demon without my permission," Aisling said, looking like she wanted to punch Owain, but her dragon was immediately there, one arm around her as he kept her at his side. "No one abuses Jim! No one!"

I thought of pointing out that the Akasha, while a plane of imprisonment, wasn't actually a place of abuse, but decided that it was better if the dragons realized they couldn't mess with Owain without repercussion.

"I have not harmed your demon," Owain said, and would have said more, but at that moment, Aisling thinned her lips at him and said, "Effrijim, I summon thee."

The demon appeared, its eyes huge as it looked from her to Owain. "Er ..."

Owain, holding Aisling's gaze, flicked his fingers, and Jim was gone again.

"Oh!" Aisling said in a near shout, her hands dancing in the air as she threw several wards on Owain.

He looked down at his chest where the wards glowed briefly before dissolving. "Binding wards?" he asked, his eyebrows rising.

To my astonishment, he plucked one of the wards off his body, causing it to become visible again, and then with a tightening of his jaw, he ground the ward into nothing.

Aisling's eyes widened in shock even as the male dragons drew in around her. "What did—you can't—did you crush my ward into smithereens?"

Owain looked at her for a few seconds before saying, "I am a thane. I can crush more than wards."

Then he did the ultimate in mic drops, and turned on his heel to enter the barn with the vampires.

The dragons, collectively, looked a bit stunned.

"He utterly destroyed my ward," Aisling said to Drake, obviously hoping for some explanation. "He didn't break it—he completely obliterated it! No one has ever done that. I didn't know it was even possible. And how does he have the ability to banish Jim to the Akasha? He's not a demon lord."

"Maybe you guys will have a little more respect for Owain," I told them all, not feeling particularly kindly toward the way they were treating him. "He may not be a demigod dragon, but he's not a pushover."

"No," Yrian said, his gaze on Becket. "He is not. I would suggest keeping the demon away from him, if for no other reason than I believe we will need Owain's goodwill. Let us have the sporting, and then we will discuss the blood moon again."

"Fine, but I'm not leaving Jim in the Akasha when it hasn't done anything wrong," Aisling said, pulling out her phone. "I'm going to see if Amelie will take it for the day."

I was about to enter the barn when a voice suddenly assaulted my ears.

"—and left me to travel the whole of the effing Beyond to find him, which is beyond infuriating. Owain! Where are you hiding, you gormless bastard! Oh, great, the knocker is still here. You, Bartleby—"

"It's Berengaria, but my friends call me Berry. You, however, can use Berengaria," I told the raven Orla when she flapped wildly over the house, making a (crooked due to her wonky wing) beeline to me. To my horror, she landed on my head, the nails of her claws digging through my knit hat and scratching my scalp. I threw my arms up in an attempt to dislodge her. "Ack! Get off me!"

"I mean … we had no intention of offending you, and I'm sorry that you feel we aren't friends—" Aisling started to say, her eyes on Orla.

"No, no, that wasn't intended for you. Dammit, Orla, get off my head! Owain is inside the barn. Go sit on him, instead."

"I will, but only because you have appalling taste in hats," she responded, and, flapping her wings in a manner that made sure they whapped me in the eyes a couple of times, took flight and headed into the building.

"What on earth?" Ysolde asked as she and Aisling looked after Orla.

"She's tied to Owain," I explained. "She tried to kill him several times because he wouldn't sleep with her, which resulted in having to curse her to get her to stop. Somehow, she ended up bound to him, and blights his existence, or at least so he said yesterday."

"Were you talking to her?" Aisling asked, glancing at her phone when it burbled at her.

"I'm a knocker," I reminded her. "We talk to birds."

"I never knew I wanted to be able to do that, but now I kind of do," Allie said as she and Ysolde entered the barn.

"Same," Ysolde said. "I've always wondered what birds say to each other."

"Mostly, they brag a lot," I told them, then asked Aisling, "I assume your demon is all right?"

"Yes," she said abruptly, her eyes tinged with ire. "No thanks to your boyfriend. Luckily, I have a friend who I've given power over Jim, and she summoned it to her house to spend the night, but I'd really appreciate it if Owain didn't mess with Jim again."

"Maybe you should rethink how superior you guys are over Owain," I told her, my own temper frayed. I took two steps, then stopped, sighed to myself, and turned back to face her. "I'm sorry, that came out a lot ruder than I intended. But you dragons are wrong for insisting Owain has no valid reason for wanting the blood moon in his hands."

Aisling opened her mouth to argue, then took me by surprise by bursting into laughter and taking my arm as she steered me toward the barn door. "You're right, but not for the reason you think. Wyverns can be the stubbornest beings alive, but luckily, they're here with us, the mates, and we bring common sense to all situations. Why don't we set aside discussions about Desi and his relic for a bit. I promise no one will seriously hurt Owain during the beatdown, and he'll most likely enjoy himself. The vamps do."

The barn had been decorated with a bunch of Christmas lights, as well as large foam and inflatable Santas, elves, candy canes, and reindeer. A couple of sturdy center wooden columns held up a loft area, now wrapped in red-and-white-striped padding, topped with a spiral of lights. In the main part of the barn, a maze of what appeared to be cubicle walls was set up, also decorated.

Owain put Orla on top of a stack of crates, arguing with her that she needed to stay out of his way.

"We are now six," Yrian said, frowning at the cubicle maze. "Should we clear the floor and have normal sporting, or do you wish for the lights to be turned out so that we can use the maze?"

"Fine, but don't come crawling to me asking for help when you're on your knees in supplication." Orla came as close to snarling as a raven could when Owain moved away.

He gave a brief martyred eye roll and told her, "Have you ever seen me on my knees in supplication?"

The men all stared at him.

"There's always a first time," Orla said with an offended sniff, and proceeded to pace back and forth across the crates, muttering rude things under her breath.

"Owain can talk to birds, too?" Aisling asked me.

"It's a family thing," I answered while the men held a brief discussion, deciding quickly that they didn't need the maze. It was dismantled and stacked in a corner; then the men returned, only to begin disrobing, each man handing his mate valuables like phones and rings, while they also shucked their winter coats and, to my surprise, their suit coats, shirts, sweaters, or any other garment worn on their upper half.

Owain hesitated for a moment, but I held out a hand. He had laid his long wool duster over a chair, but gave me a little nod as he handed me his phone and a signet ring he wore on his pinkie, and, after a moment's thought, pulled from around his neck a small round metal disk about the size of a fifty-cent piece threaded with a leather thong.

"My talisman!" Orla croaked, bobbing up and down a couple of times. "Give that to me!"

"Under no circumstances are you to do so," Owain warned me, bending a stern look on Orla, who continued to swear softly to herself.

I tucked it into my pocket, my gaze locked on him when he pulled off his shirt. The memory of his naked body remained high on my list of favorite things to recall, but an abstracted side of my mind wondered if I hadn't allowed my lust to overenhance how physically impressive he was, and how much I wanted to explore that magnificent body.

He laid his shirt on top of the coat draped on the chair, and when he turned back, I seemed to lose the ability to breathe.

"Goddess above," I murmured to myself, my eyes huge as I tried to take in his chest and arms, and the little ripple of muscle that went down his belly. He didn't have a ton of body hair, just enough to make me feel warm and wobbly inside.

"Hmm?" Ysolde, who had been holding her dragon's suit coat and shirt, turned to me. Her gaze slid past me to Owain as he listened to something Christian explained about the fighting. "Oh, my. Yes. I see what you mean."

"Amelie has Jim, so all is well there," Aisling said as she tucked her phone away. "Now we can—holy moly!" She, too, sent admiring glances toward Owain.

"He's taken, so you can stop ogling him," someone said in a voice etched with acid. To my horror, I realized it was me, and immediately put a hand over my mouth for a few seconds before I spread my fingers and apologized. "I had no idea my mouth was going to say that. Please accept my apologies."

To my relief, the ladies smiled.

"You're new to this, so no one blames you for being worried. And so you don't get upset, our policy is to look, but not touch, not even Baltic's famed six-pack that Yrian has recently given a run for his money. Oh, lord, that sentence got out of control, grammatically speaking, but I'm sure you understand," Aisling said with a little pat on my arm.

"Oooh," Allie said, catching sight of Owain's chest. "I see what you mean."

"*Kincsem,*" Drake said with an obvious warning in his eyes that had Aisling blowing him a kiss.

"I know, I know, you don't even like us looking, but come on! If you guys are going to strut around looking like male models, then you can accept a little admiration. You don't see Baltic having a hissy over Ysolde admiring his brother's six-pack."

Baltic, who had been glowering at Drake, suddenly adopted a noble mien, while Ysolde, who hadn't even been looking at Yrian, pursed her lips at her dragon. "That's because Baltic knows I love him beyond all reason. Plus, it's really Yrian's back tattoo that I admire the most."

Becket's expression turned profoundly smug as she tidied up Yrian's shirt and coat. "It really is magnificent, not that the rest of the dragons and vamps aren't up to that standard. Ladies, shall we go to the loft area? It'll have better viewing, and I have dragon's blood up there."

Owain nodded when I glanced toward him, obviously understanding my reluctance to leave him surrounded by dragons who didn't care about him, and vampires who apparently had conflicted interests. I hesitated, my stomach doing excited flip-flops when he marched over to me, his hands on my arms as he leaned close to say, "I appreciate your concern, but I do not believe this is an ambush."

I slid my glance toward Yrian, who I felt was our biggest threat of all the people present. "Are you sure?"

To my delight, he smiled, the laugh lines around his eyes crinkling in a way that had me regretting the fact that I'd turned down his offer of lovemaking the night before. Dear goddess, the man was gorgeous, but more impressive was the fact that he was there despite disagreeing with the others. He wasn't the hothead they seemed to believe; he was clearly open to listening to reason, to weighing his actions before coming to a decision.

"I'm sure." His smile grew cheeky, his eyes now back to their ringed pale gray. "I believe they truly do not know what a thane is."

"*I* know," Yrian said without even glancing our way.

We both looked at him, and I couldn't help but laugh as I said to Owain, "Aisling warned me. OK, I withdraw my concern. Have fun beating up everyone with your fabulous thaneness," I said, and leaned forward to plant a good-luck kiss on his cheek.

He froze; then suddenly I was plastered all over his chest, his arms holding me tight as his mouth pressed surprisingly gentle kisses along my lips.

I swear I about melted against him, my body turning boneless as I parted my lips, allowing him full access.

He didn't just kiss me; he took possession of my mouth, tasting me and urging me to taste him, as well. A sense of wanting, of bone-deep need, settled over me.

It was a foreign emotion, but at the same time so familiar that I felt it a part of me.

"Great. Now I'm going to have the gigantic knocker hanging around, distracting him when he should be releasing me from this freakin' curse. Well, I won't have it! I won't have it at all, do you hear?" Orla stomped back and forth along the top of the crate.

"Can you send her to the Akasha?" I murmured against Owain's lips.

"Yes, but she is so unpleasant after I retrieve her, it's not worth the respite," he answered, his eyes searching mine for something.

"Unpleasant?" Orla screeched, her voice rising at least an octave. "*Unpleasant!* You have no idea of how unpleasant I can make your life, thane!"

We both ignored her as she continued to pace across the crate top, bitching, but it was Owain who held my attention. I didn't want to examine the wad of my tangled emotions concerning him, and managed to slide out of his embrace, but not before whispering, "Tonight."

Arousal turned his eyes dark, and I may have allowed myself to climb the steep wooden staircase to the loft area with a bit more hitch in my get-along than was normal.

"I wonder if that's tantamount to the claiming of a mate?" Ysolde asked the others, scooting down a wooden bench dotted with cushions so I could join her.

"Could be," Aisling answered, studying me for a moment before smiling. "If you do end up with Owain, let us know. We have a 'mates and others' chat group where we keep in touch, and we'd be happy to add you."

"OK," I said, a little taken aback. I didn't know what else to say to that.

"What is the bird saying?" Allie asked as she sat with Tatiana on another bench. "Oooh, champagne. You've learned well, Becket!"

"Nothing worth repeating," I said, glad when Orla ran out of steam and flew in her lopsided manner around the barn, landing on an exposed rafter.

A faint rumble in the distance had me turning my head to listen. I couldn't imagine a storm had rolled in so quickly when the weak winter sun was out earlier, but the sound of thunder was unmistakable.

Becket, who had been handing out glasses of champagne, leaned over the loft railing and reminded everyone of the rules. "You guys have ten minutes. Nothing but fists, and since we don't have Gabriel present to heal people, keep in mind that if you get hurt, you have no one to blame but yourselves. Ready? And ... go!"

The men, who had spread around the room in a circle, all rushed forward toward the center ... all but Owain.

He had turned to look in the same direction as me, his head slightly cocked as he, too, was trying to catch the sound of thunder.

Drake and Baltic took his distraction to try to tackle him, but right as they rushed him, he lifted a hand, and to my utmost surprise, they stopped and looked at him in confusion.

Behind them, Christian and Finch had ganged up on Yrian.

"What is it?" Baltic asked, clearly understanding that something wasn't right.

I set down my champagne and stood up, moving over to the window high on the loft wall.

"What's wrong?" Aisling and Ysolde asked at the same time.

Something in their voices must have gotten through to the men, because the others stopped fighting and quickly got to their feet.

I held my breath for a minute, then caught the faintest hint of words carried on the frosty wind.

"Owain!" I dashed to the stairs, almost falling down them in my haste to get to him. "They're coming!"

"The Morrigna," he said in a tone that had goose bumps rippling down both of my arms.

"Who or what is a Morrigna?" Drake asked, glancing up at where Aisling leaned over the railing asking what was going on.

"Get the women to the house," Owain said, taking me by the hand, Orla swooping down and clutching the bare flesh of his shoulder as he ran for the door of the barn.

"It's his mom and her sisters," I called to the others over my shoulder. "They want to capture Owain and imprison him again."

I'll give the dragons and the vampires credit—when they needed to, they acted without question. We hadn't taken more than three steps outside the barn when the others burst out of it, the women being hustled toward the house.

"We are not weaklings who have to be protected," I heard Aisling protest. "I can help!"

"We don't know how dangerous Owain's mother is," Drake answered, more or less stuffing her into the house via a side door before following us to the front.

"It's more than just my mother," Owain said, swinging me behind him as we turned the corner to the front side of the house. "She's called on Clan Cailitin to help."

"Oh, shite!" Orla said, and, to my surprise, flew onto the roof, where she hid behind a chimney.

"Why do I have a feeling this is going to be bad?" I asked Owain, peering around his shoulder to watch the black cloud that was moving toward us at an extremely fast rate. Carried before it, the cries of, "The Morrigna, the Morrigna comes!" grew with each second.

"Because it will be." He turned around to face the semicircle of dragons and vampires behind him. "This is not your fight. Stay with your women. The Morrigna has no cause to harm them or you, but the sons of Cailitin are not to be trusted. They live for war, and care not whom it is against."

Baltic actually smiled, pulling from his pocket a small blue crystal. "If we can't fight Dark Ones, then druids will do in their place."

The front door opened, and Aisling and Ysolde emerged, both looking annoyed.

"Some people keep forgetting what a Guardian savant is—holy merde, are those birds?" Aisling stopped next to Drake, her gaze on the growing cloud of black shapes flying toward us.

"Ravens," Owain said, his eyes assessing Aisling. "Clan Cailitin has a sympathetic link to them, as well. Berry—"

"No," I said, knowing full well that he was going to ask me to go into the house with the others. "I'm a knocker. There's not much they can do to me."

"Other than remove your head," he answered, his lips twisting slightly before he said, "But I believe your point is valid. We are stronger together than apart."

I was a bit startled by that supposition, but decided now was not the time to discuss what sounded perilously like relationship talk, and instead nodded. "I wish I had my bow. I used to be a pretty good archer when I was in college."

"Luckily, Yrian likes to be prepared," Becket said as she emerged from the house with an armful of various weapons, mostly bladed. Finch and Christian, who had stopped by the latter's car, returned with two large swords. "And I did archery at college, too. We have a couple of bows, if you'd like to use one. Yrian added some magical oomph to the arrows, so they should work pretty well."

I took the offered bow, one eye on the approaching birds while tightening the bowstring, and slipped a full quiver over my shoulder.

"Weapons? Excellent. They will help." Owain looked interested as Yrian handed out weapons to the dragons, all but Baltic.

"One-handed sword, or two?" Yrian asked Owain with a politeness that, given our dire situation, made an inner giggle rise. I quelled it immediately with a quick look at the sky.

"I'll take the bastard sword, and morning star," he answered, looking through the remaining weapons.

"Dual wielding," Yrian said with a nod, and hefted a massive two-handed sword. "I prefer the damage of a good long sword, myself."

In the meantime, Drake was arguing with Aisling, but he stopped when she threatened, "You want me to set your hair on fire in front of the others? I will if you don't stop acting macho because you think dragons have something to prove to Owain. I'm not going to put myself at risk, Drake. I have faith in you and the others to keep us all safe. Calm your ta-tas, and stand in front of me so I can cast wards safely, without you having a rage stroke."

I didn't have time to watch what was obviously a battle between them, because at that moment, the first of the heralds arrived, spinning above our heads in a circle approximately fifteen feet wide.

"The Morrigna, the Morrigna!" they chanted.

Owain twirled the sword with one hand, showing off a little. I decided he deserved to do so, if for no other reason than I could feel a sense of confidence in him that I hoped boded well. "If you wish to fight, I suggest that Yrian and Baltic stand with me, and the rest of you can handle any attackers who make it past us."

There were some rumblings of disagreement from Drake and the vampires, but just as the main part of the raven swarm arrived, the men fell into place behind Owain, pushing me, Aisling, and Ysolde back against the house, protected by what was basically a wall of half-naked, extremely buff, armed men.

At the window, I could see the remaining women, their faces tight with worry.

The door opened behind me, and before I could respond, Becket grabbed me and pulled me inside, saying, "Come upstairs with me. We can shoot from the bedroom window."

I didn't argue; I raced after her up the stairs, and into a room done with gold silk Asian wall treatments, taking one of the two windows, while she—also armed with a bow—took the other.

When I flung up the sash and leaned out to look down on the others, the ravens dropped to the ground, changing into human form as they did so.

I had a moment of envy, saying under my breath, "I always play druids in video games for the shape-shifting, but dammit, now I wish I was one for real."

"Eh, dragons can shift. Yrian's form is really impressive, so I doubt if the druids have anything on him," Becket said, nocking an arrow as Jerry pushed past what appeared to be at least twenty men, all of whom had dark blond hair.

Behind her, one of her sisters followed. I didn't see the third, but decided I'd focus on the woman who'd employed me.

"Owain ap Aidan," Jerry said loudly, her voice ringing with a quality that I found hard to define. Next to her, the woman Owain had called Macha stood silent and watchful.

I ignored her and sighted Jerry, deciding to go for a leg. I didn't want to try to kill her—not that I thought I could with only a bow—but didn't have the same qualms about hobbling her.

"Before the Sons of Cailitin, I declare the time of repayment is upon you. You will return the boon lent to you, or you will be destroyed."

"Angharad ferch Cailitin," Owain said, giving another one of those braggadocio sword twirls, "in front of my twenty-seven uncles—"

"It's twenty-one, actually," the nearest druid interrupted, gesturing to the others. "The other six of the Clan are in Scotland, protecting a forest from greedy developers."

"I had to leave them to come down here," a second son said, shooting a not very friendly glance toward Jerry. "And I was in charge of the evening's entertainment. We were going to have a ceilidh, and I was going to dance with the owner of the local pub. She has plentiful breasts, and loves me to drizzle warm marmalade over her belly before I lick it off."

Silence followed that admission.

Jerry pierced her marmalade-licking brother with a look that would have skewered a mortal to the wall, then returned her focus to Owain.

"No," he simply said, obviously deciding to forgo all the formal declarations.

Jerry smiled. "As you will."

I pulled back on the bowstring, waiting for the right moment to let the arrow loose, but to my horror, instead of charging Owain, Jerry and her sister exploded into what appeared to be a couple of dozen ravens whom swarmed and completely surrounded him until all I could see was a massive moving cyclone of ravens.

The druids, most of whom were armed with staves, swept forward past the raven-covered Owain, some casting spells at the dragons and vampires, while others engaged in physical contact.

Next to me, Becket's bowstring sang as she pumped arrow after arrow into the attacking druids, while on the ground, Yrian and Baltic were in full first-line defense mode. I would have thought that their swords would make short work of wooden staves, and I suspected by the expressions of confusion on their respective faces, they thought the same.

They were wrong. In that moment, I realized why Owain was so concerned about his mother bringing her brothers to the fight. They weren't a bunch of tree-loving druids waving around staves—they had some serious magic flowing through their veins, and it splashed out in front of them, causing Yrian and Baltic to leap backward to avoid being caught in it.

I didn't hesitate. I spun around and ran out of the bedroom, leaping down the stairs in a manner that should have ended up with me breaking my neck, but I was powered by fear, worry, and fury, so by the time I hit the entrance hall floor, I was in full fight mode. I stopped at the door, and let loose a rapid volley of arrows between Aisling and Ysolde, who were casting wards and arcane balls, respectively. I shot seven druids, the arrows piercing their chests with a faint golden glow that I honestly didn't expect would do much damage.

I was mistaken in the potency of the magic with which Yrian had laced the arrows. The druids whom I picked off in their attack on Baltic and Yrian exploded in a shower of light that caused those nearest them to pause.

But my gaze was on Owain as I pushed past Aisling and Ysolde and threw myself on the raven-covered Owain, an arrow clutched in my hand, stabbing wildly into the spinning, twisting black forms. I wasn't sure which one contained Jerry's essence, but I figured sooner or later I'd find her. The shadow versions of her and Macha's raven selves dissolved into nothing as I stabbed them, gradually revealing Owain beneath. He'd been frozen, as if the Jerry swarm had turned him to stone, and to my horror, I could feel him being drained by her, the fine hairs on my arms standing on end in response.

She was taking away his power, everything that kept him safe from being imprisoned again.

He didn't deserve such treatment. He'd changed how he thought, realized the mistakes he'd made in the past, and served his penance. It wasn't right that his own mother cared so little for him that she could strip from him everything he was, and discard his broken, empty form into a convenient prison.

"Not while I still have a breath to draw," I swore as I tried to clear more ravens off him.

"This is bullshit!" one of the ravens said, immediately shifting back to human form, holding her side, which I'd evidently grazed because she didn't poof into a gold light like the druids I had nailed in the chest. She glared first at me, then at Jerry. "I don't have a horse in this battle, and I'm not going to stay and get destroyed solely because you have a beef with your son."

No one stopped her as she hurried out of the fray, not even the druids.

Instead, they let out a battle cry that hurt my ears. From the corner of my eye, I saw Yrian had shifted into the form of a smoky gray dragon, a wave of fire boiling out of him that he directed into the druids.

I was almost sobbing with fear and frustration as I kept stabbing at the Jerry-ravens, one after another dissolving into nothing when the arrow skewered their shadow forms. There were about ten left, and as I raised my hand to jab at the nearest one, it suddenly turned its head and snarled at me. "You traitor!"

"Pot, kettle, black," I said in a near growl, about to plunge the magicked arrow dead in Jerry's raven chest, but she spat out a word that sounded very old, sending me flying backward.

I hit the stone wall of the house with a crunching sound that would have made me wince had I not been almost knocked insensible. For a few seconds, pandemonium reigned about me, waves of Yrian's fire taking down druids on one side, while on the other, Baltic wielded a sword that glowed with blue light. Behind them, Drake and the two vampires were handily lopping off arms and legs of the druids who bypassed the first defense. Aisling threw wards everywhere: some protective, which drifted onto the dragons, and some prohibitive that bound the druids' feet to the ground, leaving them impotent with rage as they threatened her.

A roar ripped the air, and suddenly Owain was free of the raven swarm, his eyes blazing with a cold, pale light as he threw Jerry aside, leaping over fallen druids to pull me up into his arms, his body warm and solid and so comforting that, for a moment, I sagged against him in relief, but as I was about to push myself back, Jerry—now in her human form—rose up behind him, a wicked-looking, heavily runed and scribed silver dagger clutched in her hand.

She raised the dagger high, obviously about to pierce the back of Owain's head.

"Nooo!" The word tore from my throat in a scream unlike any I'd ever made, and without thinking, I slammed both hands into Owain's chest, throwing into the gesture every iota of energy I had, sending him stumbling backward a couple of feet.

It was enough. Jerry's blade swung downward, barely missing him, but slicing down my arm with a burning pain that almost brought me to my knees.

Owain screamed an oath in what I thought might be Welsh, dropping both his sword and the morning star, raising one fist to the air. "Orla!"

"About time," the raven said as she flew down from her perch on the roof, landing on his hand, hopping quickly onto his shoulder. "Give him my talisman, you idiot knocker. He needs it."

I tried to lift my hand to get the metal disk from my pocket, but my arm hung limply, not responding to my commands.

"You stupid bint," Jerry said, jumping when Yrian directed a wave of fire at her. "I should have known better than to hire an apprentice." She leaped toward Owain in a suitably dramatic manner, the bloodstained dagger raised high again.

I got the disk with my working arm right at the moment that time seemed to telescope, stretching out in a way that had Owain's turn to face his mother slowed, my hand moving at a snail's pace as I reached above his head, allowing the leather thong bearing the talisman to slide down until it settled around his neck.

The second it touched his bare flesh, he slammed his hands forward, palms out, white light channeled directly into Jerry. A look of utter surprise crossed her face for a moment; then she was gone, as if she'd blinked out of existence.

"Now, that's what I'm talking about, some good old-fashioned banishment," Orla said, hopping up and down excitedly. "Do it again! Send all those freaks of nature to the Akasha!"

The druids nearest us paused. As a group, they looked at the spot where a second before, Jerry was about to seriously harm her son. Then they looked at Owain, Orla, and finally me.

I lifted my bow.

"Er …" The nearest druid cleared his throat.

Baltic and Yrian, both panting, lowered their weapons, while one last arcane ball zipped past my ear to hit an unlucky druid in the face.

He went down with a squawk.

"Yeah, I'm out of here, too. My wife wasn't happy I left her with the kids to answer Jerry's call, and you never want to piss off an earth fury if you can help it," another druid said, before giving Owain a half smile. "Glad to see you're doing well, Owain. When did you get out of the Hour? Never did think it was right that you were put there. Your brothers, yes, they're batshit crazy, as my youngest would say, but you always seemed to be decent, and much more reasonable than them. Welp, brothers, shall we?"

"What about the others?" the druid with the pub owner girlfriend asked, gesturing to the bodies of the fallen.

"Eh. Da will bring them back. He always does," the first one answered, then, with an apologetic smile at the rest of us, gave a little wave, turned into a raven, and immediately flew off.

"This was fun, but as Flann said, I have things to do. Later, all," another druid said.

The rest of the druids murmured similar excuses, and in a few seconds, they'd all left.

I touched Owain on the arm, pulling his attention from glaring at the sky to me. "What did you do to your mother?"

"What you suggested," he answered, frowning when Orla hopped onto his head. He lifted her off, setting her on a stone planter next to the door before examining my arm. It still hurt, but was already starting to heal.

I dug through my memory of the last half hour, but came up blank. "What did I say?"

"You mentioned sending Orla to the Akasha—"

"That bitch!" Orla said on a birdy gasp. "She did? Well, I know whose head I'm going to poop on the very next time I have the chance. And I'll be sure to eat a bunch of berries first, so it's nice and seedy, and extra runny!"

"—so I sent my mother there. It seemed like the best way to get her to leave us alone until we find the blood moon," he finished, ignoring Orla. "She'll get herself out eventually, but it takes longer to get out of the Akasha than the Beyond, so we should have at least a few weeks of peace before she does so."

I smiled, using my nonhurt hand to wipe blood from a scratch on the side of his face, aware of, but not paying attention to, the dragons and vampires who were tidily stacking up the bodies of the (evidently temporarily) dead druids against the side of the house. "That is the perfect solution, and you know that I'll do everything I can to help you."

"You already have," he said, pulling me up against his bare chest. For a moment, I hesitated, testing my emotions to see if we were go for everything that I badly wanted to do to, and with, him, and getting the go-ahead, I tipped my head back to kiss him.

"Oooh, he has his soul back. Nice job, Berry," Allie said, emerging with a bunch of coats and shirts in her arms, handing them out to the men.

For the next four minutes, I paid no mind to anything but allowing my libido to unleash itself in kissing Owain, the sense of him sinking into my veins, filling me with a sense of rightness.

"I'm in so much trouble," I whispered against his lips.

"Why?" he asked, his eyes pale as the winter moon, but at the same time so full of warmth, I almost felt like stripping down.

Or perhaps that was just the feeling of his skin beneath my hands.

"Because I'm going to fall madly in love with you, and then I'll have the mother-in-law from hell."

"Literally," Aisling said with a laugh as she and the others entered the house, leaving us alone with Yrian and Becket, both of whom were draping some tarps over the druids.

I searched Owain's face, asking softly, "What did Allie mean about your soul?"

He hesitated for a few seconds, then said slowly, "Many Dark Ones are born without souls, which can only be redeemed by their Beloveds, what you would call soulmates."

"OK," I said. "But you aren't a vampire."

"No, but when Desislav and the others laid the bloodlust curse upon us, they took our souls as punishment. It was part of the curse that was passed down to our descendants."

"I doubt it was Desi who insisted on you forfeiting your souls," Yrian said as he and Becket walked past us to the front door. She entered, but he paused to add, "I've long suspected that Kashi had his fingers in that pie, and from what my youngest brother tells me, it is likely Kashi, not the other princes of Abaddon, who wanted the souls of you and your brothers."

Owain's lips thinned for a few seconds. "That is of some comfort, but it does not change my stance on Desislav and the blood moon."

Yrian inclined his head in acknowledgment of that statement, and entered the house, the door closing softly behind him.

I one-handedly helped Owain into his shirt and coat, ignoring Orla when she went into a detailed rant about people who want to unfairly banish helpful witches-turned-ravens.

"So you got your soul back?" I asked him. "How?"

"You sacrificed yourself for me," he answered, a slow smile raising my temperature at least five degrees. "A Beloved who does that redeems their Dark One's soul."

"I'm not a Beloved any more than you are a bloodsucking vamp," I told him, wanting, for some reason I didn't wish to examine closely, to dance and sing and kiss Owain all over his body.

"I am happy to have you do so, but only after I've taken my turn kissing your delectable self," he said, turning toward the house. "And yes, I want to feed from you."

I gave a little jerk to the side, sure I had kept that thought well hidden in the shadows of my mind. "Really? Will it … er … hurt? I don't mind the sight of blood, but I'm not a fan of pain."

His smile was made up of such lasciviousness, a blush swept up from my chest. "It won't hurt, but I promise you'll be a boneless heap of satisfied woman by the time I'm done feeding."

"Oooh," I said, a shiver of anticipation rippling down my back. "I'm going to hold you to that promise. But …" I paused, making him turn back toward me. "What are you going to do about the dragons?"

He was silent for almost a minute before heaving a heartfelt sigh. "I will treat with them."

"Huh?"

He frowned. "How old are you?"

"Eighty-two. You're going to treat them how?"

"I'm going to treat with them—negotiate. Yrian seems not unreasonable, even if the other dragons are less inclined to be so. I don't know how joint custody of the blood moon would work, but I am willing to discuss the matter with him."

Relief filled me at yet another sign that he wasn't the deranged, homicidal madman that everyone thought him. "OK, but I reserve the right to sic Orla on them if they don't play ball with you."

"Hey!" Orla shook her feathers until she was puffed up like a black hedgehog. "You don't get to tell me what to do! No one gets to do that, not even lover boy, there. I'm my own person, a powerful hedge witch, and I am not going to let you two sideline me so you can make lovey eyes at each other, and probably go shag for hours and hours and hours, leaving me all alone with no one. No, sir, Owain cursed me, so I'm going to stick with him every second of every day, if only to show you two who's really in char—"

"I really want to learn how to do that," I said after Owain, with a glance toward the fractious bird and a quick flick of his fingers, put an arm around me and escorted me into the house.

"I'll teach you," he promised, the sound of Orla's squawk as she was sent once again to the Beyond music to my ears.

EPILOGUE
EFFRIJIM

Heya, Desi, hope you don't mind a voice note. It was fun seeing you guys last night at our Boxing Day dinner, and since Aisling told me that it might help Parisi if I send her video updates on what's going on in my life, I thought I'd do that.

Today is a big day in the World of Jim, so I figured I'd share it with you both. I was going to video what I did during the whole day, but Aisling thought that might be a bit much, and since there are others here, she said it might be best to do a voice chat. So here I am, chatting.

This afternoon, Amelie rolled into the backyard of Drake's Paris house. She had Cecile's pram with her, with my delicious fuzzybutt riding in it like the queen she is, swaddled in several blankets to keep her comfy. Yrian was going to swing by and make Cecile immortal, so I asked Amelie if she was excited.

"Of course," she answered, but I noticed a bit of strain alongside her mouth.

Since Amelie is not my bestiest bestie (that would be Aisling, since Cecile is the love of my life, and that tops even Ash) but is still right up there in the heights of bestie-land, I gave her a comforting rub on the leg, until I realized I'd slimed her nice wool black skirt.

"It'll be OK," I told her, hoping she didn't notice the drool. "Yrian swore that nothing bad can happen, and there's no way Cecile will be harmed. Now that her teeth are all good, this is the best time to make sure she's with me until the stars fade from the sky."

Aisling, who somehow saw the slobber mishap, sighed and grabbed a fresh hand towel from where we had a box of them on the patio table, and scooted me aside to wipe off Amelie's skirt. "Of course nothing untoward is going to happen to Cecile. Yrian is a big animal lover, even if he does favor cats. They have llamas and goats now, as well as their three cats and Becket's pug. Jim, please mind where you place your flews."

"I'm not worried about anything bad befalling Cecile," Amelie said in her soft French accent. Did I tell you guys she was French? She is. "I regret that the day will come when we are parted, but I know that she will live on in happiness with you when that time comes."

I may have sniffled a little.

Aisling eyed me.

"Got a piece of grass up my nose," I said, blinking rapidly. "It also affects the eyes."

She gave me one of the smiles that remind me so much of my friend Camio, and hugged me before hugging Amelie, as well. "Just when I think I'm at my limit of sass from you for the day, you restore my hope in demonkind. Oh, there's Yrian and Becket. I think everyone's here, so we can get started."

I snuffled Cecile, who, since she was napping in what passed for the sun in Paris in late December, woke up a bit snappish.

"It's OK," I told her, my heart so full of happiness I thought for a moment about changing my form into a human so I could tap-dance on the patio. Then the memory returned of how horrible human form had been, and with it came sanity, so I gave the side of her face a quick slurp (you gotta be quick around her when she's snappy) and beamed at everyone.

"I hope you don't mind that we tagged along." A couple of new friends, Berry and ... er ... her boyfriend exited the house on Yrian's heels, Berry smiling at everyone as she continued, "We were in Wales so we could hash out the terms of an agreement with Yrian, and he said you wouldn't mind if we joined you all in the big goings-on."

"Of course we don't mind if you are here," Aisling said, her eyes growing a bit wide as she regarded the BF. I didn't blame her. I wasn't around to see what Berry's boyfriend did to the druids that attacked him and some of the dragons, but evidently he (and the raven who's always bitching at him) aren't peeps you want to run into in a dark alley, if you get what I'm saying.

Yrian made a bow to the ladies, 'cause he's old-school that way, and gave me less of a stink eye than was normal, so I figured it would be good if I oozed some charm on him.

"Heya, Eerie-man. How they hangin'? We're all set up here with everything you asked for, although I'm not quite sure why you need dragon's blood to make a Welsh corgi immortal," I said, doing a quick snuffle of his shoes and pant legs.

"We're so grateful you agreed to do this for Cecile and Jim," Aisling said, shooing me away from him, Drake at her side. "It's very kind of you to make sure that we don't ever have to face life without her."

"It's my pleasure," Yrian said politely, then cocked an eyebrow at Amelie. "If you desire, I can make you a dragon, and you will not be parted from your dog."

"Oh," Amelie said, her eyes growing big as she looked from him to Aisling and back. "That's … that's very kind of you, but I am happy as I am. Thank you, though."

"That really is sweet," Aisling said, her eyes almost as wide as Amelie's. "Although I didn't realize you could make people dragons, too. Drake?"

Drake was now considering Yrian. "I admit I wasn't aware that anyone could do so other than the First Dragon."

Yrian simply smiled, and reached down to pat Cecile.

"You might want to not get your hand in front of her mouth—" I started to warn him, but to my surprise—and honestly pretty much that of everyone there—Cecile didn't snap at him. In fact, she sniffed his hand, and even gave it a little lick before snuggling back into her blankies. "OK, so you're what, a corgi whisperer in addition to being a demigod dragon?"

"Animals have always liked me," he said, then addressed Amelie. "You are sure you do not wish to be a dragon? I can guarantee that you would be welcome in the weyr, either with a tribe or sept, if that is what you desire."

"I have nothing but respect for the dragonkin," Amelie said with a little smile. "But no, I will remain as I am. I do not fear my end in this world."

"As you wish," Yrian said, then after accepting a glass of the dragon's blood wine that you and Parisi tried last night (and I hope that butternut squash soup stain comes out of her dress after she barfed up the wine and soup), and everyone toasting Cecile's new beginning (as we're putting it, since Ash tears up every time she thinks about Amelie not being with us anymore), he said a few things in a language I've never heard before, but which sounded like something old.

Really, really old. I bet you'd know what it was, but since I had to rush forward as soon as he was done and check Cecile to make sure she didn't smell different, I didn't get a chance to ask about it.

Just so you don't worry, Cecile was fine afterward. She went back to sleep, and we all went inside to have a celebratory dinner.

There was one thing, though. When we were going back into the house, Yrian and Berry's BF exchanged what I can only call a knowing look. As Amelie went inside, the BF murmured something about a leaf being in her hair, and touched her briefly on her forehead as he brushed it off.

I didn't see a leaf on her head, although he had one in his hand afterward. But when he and Berry went inside, she whispered to him, "Did you do it?" and he nodded.

I had a good long look at Amelie later, after dinner, and went over to sit on the BF's foot to let him know I knew.

He tried to push me off, but I leaned back and asked, "How many years does your blessing give Amelie?"

Berry leaned forward, pinning me back with a look that almost had my hackles rising, so I got up and headed for where Cecile was snoozing on my plush dog bed.

But before I got more than two steps, the BF said softly, "The remainder of her life will be long and happy."

I smiled at him. The guy's a big softy, which considering who he is … er … yeah, that's not really important, right? Right.

Thanks for the new collar, by the way. I like how you put protection runes on it, although Aisling said it was a bit overkill to stud it with actual diamonds.

I hope you guys have a happy new year. It looks like mine is going to be … interesting.

Laters!

CALL ME, MAYBE?

My lovely one! I hope you enjoyed reading *A Vampire in a Pear Tree*, which I handcrafted from the finest artisanal words just for you. If you are new to my dragon books, and want to see more about Jim, Aisling, Drake, and other denizens of the Otherworld, feel free to dive into *You Slay Me*, the first book in the dragon series. Likewise, you could visit *A Girl's Guide to Vampires* for the first in the Dark Ones series.

Want more? Join my newsletter at katiemacalister.com for news, exclusive reader bonuses like sneak peaks, extra scenes, and bonus epilogues. It's free and fun. And full of weirdness. Admittedly, lots of weirdness…

ABOUT KATIE

Bird skeleton washer.

Doll's house salesperson to royalty.

King Tut tour guide.

Katie MacAlister has not just worked odd jobs, she's lived an even odder life. Luckily, she's always had a book with her to take her away from the weirdness.

Two years after she started writing novels, Katie sold her first romance, *Noble Intentions*. More than seventy books later, her novels have been translated into numerous languages, been recorded as audiobooks, received several awards, and have been regulars on the *New York Times*, *USA Today*, *Wall Street Journal*, and *Publishers Weekly* bestseller lists. Katie is a widow who lives in the Pacific Northwest with two dogs, and can often be found lurking around online.

You are welcome to join Katie's official discussion group on Facebook, as well as connect on Instagram and Discord. For more information, visit: katiemacalister.com